EMPTY GUN

Fargo's first bullet went into a rushing Shoshoni warrior, who went backward as if kicked by a mule.

His next two bullets went into the two white captives lying on the ground, to put them out of their pain after their savage torture.

Then Fargo finished off the three braves who came charging at him.

Now, with his gun emptied, he thought he was through—but the Shoshoni weren't. The Trailsman could see what was coming in the look on their faces and the weapons in their hands.

His certain death . . .

RIDING THE WESTERN TRAIL

☐ **THE TRAILSMAN #99: CAMP SAINT LUCIFER by Jon Sharpe.** Skye Fargo blazes away against an infernal killing crew as he follows a terror trail of corpses to a secret encampment where men kill like savages.
(164431—$3.50)

☐ **THE TRAILSMAN #100: RIVERBOAT GOLD by Jon Sharpe.** Skye Fargo steers a deathship through a rising tide of terror on the evil end of the Mississippi.
(164814—$3.95)

☐ **THE TRAILSMAN #101: SHOSHONI SPIRITS by Jon Sharpe.** Skye Fargo blazes through a maze of redskin magic and savage murder to aid a beautiful woman who leads him over the Rockies to a lot of trouble.
(165489—$3.50)

☐ **THE TRAILSMAN #103: SECRET SIXGUNS by Jon Sharpe.** Doc Emerson was missing, and his old pal, Skye Fargo, had to comb the Rockies for him. What Fargo found was a secret more evil than could ever be imagined.
(166116—$3.50)

☐ **THE TRAILSMAN #104: COMANCHE CROSSING by Jon Sharpe.** Skye Fargo faced a Mexican calvary on a campaign of carnage, Comanche warriors on a trail of lust and loot ... and a mystery shrouded by murder. A new set of players in a no-limit game.
(167058—$3.50)

☐ **THE TRAILSMAN #105: BLACK HILLS BLOOD by Jon Sharpe.** Skye Fargo faced a three-ring Wild West show of white greed and redskin savagery, complete with an exotic enchantress who charmed more than snakes.
(167260—$3.50)

☐ **THE TRAILSMAN #106: SIERRA SHOOT-OUT by Jon Sharpe.** Skye Fargo found anglo ranchers and Mexican settlers, embattled missionaries and marauding banditos, all waging a war where he couldn't tell good guys from bad without a gun.
(167465—$3.50)

THE
TRAILSMAN
110

COUNTERFEIT
CARGO

by

Jon Sharpe

A SIGNET BOOK

Penguin Group
SA Inc., 375 Hudson Street, .
York 10014, U.S.A.
Penguin Books Ltd, 27 Wrights Lane,
London W8 5TZ, England
Penguin Books Australia Ltd, Ringwood,
Victoria, Australia
Penguin Books Canada Ltd, 2801 John Street,
Markham, Ontario, Canada L3R 1B4
Penguin Books (N.Z.) Ltd, 182-190 Wairau Road,
Auckland 10, New Zealand

Penguin Books Ltd, Registered Offices:
Harmondsworth, Middlesex, England

First published by Signet, an imprint of New American Library,
a division of Penguin Books USA Inc.

First Printing, February, 1991
10 9 8 7 6 5 4 3 2 1

The first chapter of this book originally appeared in *Lone Star Lightning*,
the one hundred and ninth volume in this series.

Printed in the United States of America

PUBLISHER'S NOTE
This is a work of fiction. Names, characters, places, and incidents either
are the product of the author's imagination or are used fictitiously, and
any resemblance to actual persons, living or dead, events, or locales is
entirely coincidental.

The Trailsman

Beginnings . . . they bend the tree and they mark the man. Skye Fargo was born when he was eighteen. Terror was his midwife, vengeance his first cry. Killing spawned Skye Fargo, ruthless, cold-blooded murder. Out of the acrid smoke of gunpowder still hanging in the air, he rose, cried out a promise never forgotten.

The Trailsman, they began to call him, all across the West: searcher, scout, hunter, the man who could see where others only looked, his skills for hire but not his soul, the man who lived each day to the fullest, yet trailed each tomorrow. Skye Fargo, the Trailsman, the seeker who could take the wildness of a land and the wanting of a woman and make them his own.

*1860, where the Montana and
Idaho territories shoulder each other
along the Cabinet Mountains,
a land waiting to devour the good
and the bad alike . . .*

1

It had been that kind of a day, the big man with the lake-blue eyes muttered under his breath. The girl first, he added with a silent oath as he moved the Ovaro slowly downward, the horse's jet-black fore- and hind-quarters and white midsection glistening against the deep-green, tapering leaves of the bur oaks that dotted the hillside. The damn girl! She had shattered the peace of the morning and turned the whole damned day around. Now, instead of feeling rested and refreshed, his head still throbbed and his mouth felt as though he were chewing cotton. Skye Fargo swore again under his breath.

His thoughts reeled backward. Not far. It had only been a few hours before. He had taken off his clothes, down to almost nothing, and stretched his near-naked self out on a flat, soft bed of mountain fern moss to let the hot sun bake down on him. He had guessed it would take the entire morning and maybe a little more for the sun to sweat the bourbon out of him and stop the pounding in his head, all the result of a night of carousing in West Hollow, just east of Whitefish.

His thoughts reeled back a little further, to the night with Will and Tom Brady. It had been part reunion and part celebration. He had just brought a herd to Will and Tom that blazed a new trail up from Wind River land in Wyoming and they were all in a mood for celebrating. It had been a long, hot, and hard trek through Cheyenne and Shoshoni country, but the new trail he'd blazed was better than the old, protected and less mountainous.

It had indeed been a time for celebrating and they'd done so with a vengeance, exchanging too many stories and downing too many bourbons. They'd stayed in the dance hall in West Hollow and the girl had come to the table when the night was late. Strangely enough, he remembered her more clearly than he did much else—young, thin, pretty in a wan kind of way. He had shrugged her away at first. He was never much one for dance-hall girls. But she had stayed, pleasantly persistent, and when Tom and Will went under, Fargo found himself in a room with her. She was new to the dance hall, she told him. Maybe because of that, maybe because she was surprisingly tender with her own kind of quiet sweetness, she worked her way into his arms. She had small breasts, a little on the flat side, a thin body.

Perhaps all the bourbon helped, but she managed to generate her own sensuousness—surprising, given the lack of sensuousness in her body. She had brought the rest of the bottle along to keep the mood going and had managed to drink a good part of it herself. He didn't remember much about the rest of the night, except the lovemaking, and that only in a vague way.

The dawn had come and he pulled himself together and weaved his way from the room with a glance back at the slender girl asleep in the bed. When he reached the street outside, his head felt as though a buffalo stampede was taking place inside it. He climbed onto the Ovaro, rode from town, and headed into the low hills. He managed to ride for over an hour when he came to the patch of soft mountain fern moss in the hot sun and decided that Mother Nature's healing was his best hope.

Clothes shed, he had slept in the hot, baking sun, dimly aware he was perspiring profusely, for at least two hours, he guessed, when the clatter of hoofbeats broke the silence of the small glade. His hand was on

10

the butt of the big Colt at his side before he pulled his eyes open to see a horse being reined to a sharp halt. He blinked away sleep and the figure in the saddle took on shape, then details. He saw a young woman, dark-brown hair pulled back in a bun, a long neck, straight nose, snappingly bright blue eyes, nicely matched lips, an attractive face, though a little severely held together. She wore a white blouse buttoned to the neck, and a modest swell of breasts pushed the front out.

"Thank God," she said. "I've been riding all over to find somebody. My wagon's broken. I need help."

Skye Fargo blinked, licked his dry lips with a tongue hardly less dry, and saw her eyes take in his near nakedness with disapproval.

"Would you put on your clothes and follow me?" she said, her tone more a command than a request.

He grimaced as a particularly sharp throb of pain went through his head. "Go away, girlie," he said, and lay back on the moss. The pain in his head lessened at once and he sighed in relief.

"What did you say?" The young woman frowned.

"Go away. Forget it," Fargo said. He was to meet Jake Carmody in Loggerville by the end of the day. Sheriff Jake Carmody. He didn't aim to do that still suffering from a hangover. He needed more peace and quiet. He looked up at the young woman. "Keep riding, honey. You'll find somebody," he said, and closed his eyes. The throbbing lessened at once.

"I've been riding for hours in all directions. You're the first person I've come upon," he heard her say.

"Keep looking."

"Dammit, you've got to come with me. I've valuable cargo in my wagon."

His eyes stayed closed. "Get lost."

"You are coming with me," he heard her insist, her voice rising.

"On your way, honey. You're interrupting medical

11

treatment. I've got to rest my head," he said, his eyes staying closed.

"You mean your self-indulgent, drink-sodden body," he heard her snap.

"Whatever," he grunted. "But I'm staying right here." He heard her wheel the horse, a sudden sharp movement, and he pulled his eyes open in time to see her lean from the saddle and scoop up his trousers, shirt, and boots.

"Then you won't be needing these," she flung back as she sent the horse into a gallop.

"Goddamn," Fargo swore as he jumped to his feet, ignored the pain that shot through his head. "You come back here," he shouted, but she had already vanished into the trees. "Goddamn little bitch," Fargo swore aloud, bent over, and winced as the blood rushed through his head and brought the sharp pain with it. He picked up his gun belt, strapped it on over his drawers, and headed for the Ovaro, cursing as he stepped on a sharp piece of stone. He pulled himself into the saddle and started into the trees after her.

She had left riding hard and he didn't try to catch up to her, for every jounce sent a stab of pain through him. He followed the hoofprints of her horse up a slope that leveled off, rose again, and crested, and he moved down the far side of the slope. He spotted the wagon in a hollow along a mountain path. An Owensboro Texas wagon outfitted with top bows and canvas, rear wheels larger than the front, which made for both good traction and good steering. Almost as much room inside as in a Conestoga, he knew, and his eyes went to the young woman. She had dismounted and waited alongside the wagon, a cool appraisal in her eyes as he rode to a halt.

"My, it seems you can stir yourself," she said tartly. "All you need is the right motivation."

Fargo stayed silent as he swung from the Ovaro, sweeping her Owensboro again with a quick glance. He took in the team of solid horses hitched to the front and his eyes moved to the rear wheel, which jutted out at a crazy angle from the body of the wagon. It had gone into a deep hole and he swept the rear carriage of the wagon with a quick, experienced eye. The wheel appeared broken to the novice, but it wasn't. The hub was still on the axle skein, and he saw that the axle itself had shifted all the way to one side when the wheel went into the hole. The play was built into the gear to allow for just such moments, all designed to prevent a wheel from snapping off against a stiff, unyielding axletree.

Some axles had a little too much play in them and could cause a wheel to come loose. This was probably one of those, but in this instance it had done its job. With the right maneuver, the axle would shift back and the wheel go into place.

He paused and glanced inside the wagon to see only traveling bags and hatboxes. "This your valuable cargo?" he asked.

"Part of it," she said, unfazed.

He sauntered toward her and saw her eyes move across the muscled symmetry of his near-naked body. "The wheel's not broken," he told her. "Lift the rear of the wagon at the same time you set the team to pulling. Everything will slip back into place."

"You can help me do that right now," she said.

Fargo's smile was made of ice. "Go to hell, honey," he said as he moved closer to her.

"I can't do it by myself and you're here," she said with just a trace of smugness.

He moved a step closer before his arms shot out with the speed of a rattler's strike. He curled one hand around her waist, the other around the back of her neck, and yanked her forward. She came with a half-scream of surprise and he dropped to one knee and turned her over the other. He felt the firmness of her body as he held her with one hand pressed into her back while he brought his other palm-down real hard on her rear. Her first scream was a mixture of fury and pain. He administered at least a half-dozen stinging slaps to her rear, and her last two gasped screams were more pain than fury. He stood up and dumped her onto the ground, where he stared down at her for a moment.

"You probably should've had more of that when you were growing up," he said.

Her even lips worked for a moment before the words came. "You rotten bastard," she said as he strode away and scooped up his clothes. He turned as she regained her feet, put a hand to her rear, and drew it away at once as her lips parted in a short gasp of pain. "You are the lowest, rottenest, meanest man I've ever met," she said.

"Be glad I didn't pull your britches down," Fargo said blandly.

Her eyes were snapping darts of blue fire. "I'm surprised you didn't," she flung back tartly.

"I thought about it," he said as he walked to the Ovaro.

"What stopped you? Certainly not becoming a gentleman all of a sudden."

"I figured you for a bony, flat ass not worth the seeing," he tossed back. She didn't see his smile as he swung onto the pinto, but he saw her casting about for something to throw as he started to ride away.

"Rotten, stinking, no-good bastard," she screamed after him. He rode on without a glance back, his head pounding fiercely again. He needed another few hours of sweating in the sun, he realized, and he rode back to the flat bed of moss, stretched out once again, but kept his clothes closer this time. Arrogant little spitfire, he muttered to himself as he thought about the girl. Maybe she'd learned a lesson about high-handed behavior. He closed his eyes. He slept in minutes and let his body absorb the welcome heat of the sun's burning rays.

The afternoon had begun to move toward its end when he woke, stretched, and smiled as he felt not the hint of an ache or throb. He dressed quickly and climbed onto the pinto. It was time to head for Loggerville and Sheriff Jake Carmody. As he rode, he realized he hadn't seen Jake in at least three years. Jake had been talking about retiring then, Fargo remembered. Carmody had to be in his mid-fifties, a good, honest man, not too hard yet not intimidated, the perfect sheriff for a town such as Loggerville.

The town nestled at the foot of the Cabinet Mountains, one of the many individual mountain ranges that made up the giant sweep of the Rockies. Loggerville was a town with more than the usual share of tough, rough loggers and mountain men, some mean at heart but most only mean by liquor. Yet there were plenty of men on the run who stopped at a town such as Loggerville while they decided whether to dare the wild fastness of the mountains or turn and flee in another direction.

Fargo turned the Ovaro along the hillside where he had pursued the young woman. It was on his way north and he reached the hollow and the path to find the wagon gone. Someone had come along and helped her, or she'd gone out and found someone else. Either way she had managed, and he wasn't surprised at that. Not with her talent for concocting a story about valuable cargo and her spitfire determination.

Now that he'd rid himself of his stupendous hangover and his own anger had died down, he found himself curious about her. What was a dammed attractive young woman doing in these wild foothills all alone in a big Texas mountain wagon? he wondered. She was quick-minded as well as quick-tempered. He'd learned that in the few brief moments he'd been with her. And one thing more . . . He smiled. Her ass hadn't been at all flat and bony under his hand. But he pushed further thoughts about her from his mind. He had to get to Loggerville and Jake Carmody.

That had been the morning, and his thoughts had come full circle. And now this, Fargo swore as he threaded his way down the hillside. The figure lay facedown at the bottom of the slope, his hat still on. Fargo swore under his breath. Only one man that he knew of wore that hat, an extra-large-brimmed, white stetson with a tan band. Jake Carmody.

Fargo's eyes swept the bur oaks that spread along both sides of the bottom of the slope, but he saw nothing move. He spurred the pinto into a trot and reached the bottom of the hill, where he landed on the balls of his feet before the horse came to a halt.

He dropped to one knee beside Jake's burly figure. Jake was alive, he quickly saw with relief, his breathing steady. He turned the sheriff over and saw the bloody gash along the side of his temple. He pushed the wide-brimmed stetson from Jake's head, took a kerchief and water from his canteen, and applied the cold compress to the wound. He repeated the compress four times, then he saw the sheriff's eyes slowly come open, stare up at him, and finally the blankness in them filled with recognition.

"Jesus, Fargo . . . How'd you get here?" Jake Carmody asked.

"Just what I was going to ask you." Fargo said.

The older man pushed himself up on one elbow and winced at the pain. "Old age, that's how, goddammit," Jake Carmody said. He paused and took in Fargo's questioning frown. "I was bringing two prisoners back when they jumped me," Jake explained. "One of them made a funny motion and I pulled my gun on him when the other one hit me from the back. My own damn fault. I let them sucker me into it. Even so, ten years ago I'd have been quick enough to avoid it. Maybe even five years ago. But not now." The older man started to rise and fell back in pain. "Jesus, guess I twisted my leg when I fell," he said.

"Stay right here. Rest yourself. I'll get them back for you," Fargo said.

Jake Carmody's eyes lighted with gratitude. "Would you, old friend?" he said. "I sure as hell can't do it.

They took my gun and horse with them. Two weasly range rats wanted for murderin' an old trapper and stealin' his pelts. The tall one's Boyd Royce, the short one's Enoch Cable."

"Stay right here. Lay back and rest. Keep the cold compress against your head," Fargo said as he rose and swung onto the Ovaro.

"Watch yourself, Fargo. They're not going to take to coming back with you," the sheriff said.

"That'll be their choice," Fargo said grimly, and moved the pinto in a slow circle until he spotted the hoofprints, three horses moving north. With a wave back at Jake, he rode on and followed the fresh prints with ease.

They had raced away, hoofmarks dug deep into the soil, but then slowed, Fargo noted. They stayed at a leisurely pace, plainly confident Jake wouldn't be following after them. The prints swung into a forest of red ash and emerged to move down to a narrow path along a low plateau dotted with box elder.

Fargo stayed on the low hill and finally spotted them as they rode side by side with Jake's horse following behind. Though both wore gun belts, they had only one gun, Jake's, and Fargo saw it on the hip of the tall figure. Boyd Royce, Jake had called him, and he sat a full head taller than his companion.

Fargo moved the pinto slowly along the top of the low hill, through a line of young cottonwoods. He stayed there as he passed the two riders below. He wanted to avoid coming up behind them—and precipitate a chase that could lose at least one on him. When he was some two hundred yards beyond the duo, he turned the pinto downward and was casually riding along the path when the two men caught up to him. He half-turned in the saddle as the two riders came closer, allowed a friendly smile that took in both men.

" 'Afternoon, gents," Fargo said, and saw both men regard him with the kind of expression a fox views a chicken. He let them draw to a halt, and when he turned back again, the big Colt was in his hand. "Drop the gun, Boyd," he growled, and the tall man's eyes widened in surprise. "Nice and slow," he added.

Boyd stared at him as he slowly lifted the gun from the holster and let it drop to the ground. "Who the hell are you, mister?" Royce growled.

"Sheriff Carmody sent me," Fargo said. Both men shot glances of astonishment at each other. "He was sorry you left without even saying good-bye. Bad manners. You'll have to come back and stay after school. Get off your horses. You first, Boyd." The man slid from the saddle under Fargo's gaze. "You next," Fargo ordered the shorter figure.

"You're smarter than the old man," Boyd Royce muttered.

"Step back, away from the horses," Fargo said, and both men obeyed. He waited till they were back far enough to lower the Colt for a moment as he leaned forward and took hold of the reins of both horses, then he backed the pinto and tied the reins to the saddle horn of Jake's horse. "You boys are going to walk back," he said. "It'll take all the extra energy out of you."

He half-turned to pull the horses facing the same direction when he caught the faint sound, fabric being brushed aside. He whirled just in time to see the shorter one, Enoch Cable, yank the gun out from inside his shirt. He flung himself sideways from the saddle as the man fired, but he felt the sharp, searing pain along the top of his forehead.

He hit the ground on his back as he shook away a wave of fog that tried to settle over him; he managed to roll and heard another shot slam into the ground inches from his head. The fog tried to descend on him again. He shook his head and it lifted in time for him to see Cable rushing at him, the gun upraised. He managed to kick out, the blow landing squarely in the man's groin and the figure doubled up in a curse of pain.

Fargo rolled, brought his gun hand up to fire, and with a curse realized that his hand was empty. The Colt had fallen from his grip when he hit the ground, and he spied it in the grass a dozen feet away. He also saw Boyd Royce racing to pounce on it and he flung himself forward. He reached the gun just as Boyd did, and the Trailsman closed one hand around the man's wrist. He yanked, but Royce kept his grip on the butt of the pistol and Fargo rolled sideways and took the tall figure with him.

Out of the corner of his eye he glimpsed Enoch Cable, one hand still holding his groin, start to pull himself to his feet. Royce tried to wrestle his wrist free, but Fargo's grip was viselike, and he arched his back, rolled again, and took the man with him. This time he twisted hard on Royce's wrist and the man swore in pain as the Colt fell from his fingers. Fargo released his grip and scooped up the revolver as Royce wrestled himself free. The man half-rolled, half-dived along the ground, but Fargo's eyes were on Cable, who was coming toward him with the gun in his hand. Fargo fired two shots from the Colt, his arm resting on the ground, and Enoch Cable shuddered, staggered sideways, and collapsed.

Fargo spun to see Boyd Royce scooping up Jake Carmody's gun. He fired the Colt as Royce whirled on him, and the man's tall body straightened out as he flew backward, a small fountain of red spurting from his chest. He hit the ground and lay still, and Fargo rose to his feet, holstered the Colt, and moved from the short figure to the tall one as he picked up both guns. He stared at the gun Enoch had pulled from inside his shirt. If he'd had it all along, why hadn't he pulled it on the sheriff? And if he didn't have it then, where did he get it?

Tabling the questions, Fargo lifted each man face-down across his horse and climbed onto the Ovaro to lead the silent procession back the way he'd come.

Dusk had begun to settle over the hills when he

reached the spot where Jake Carmody waited, sprawled atop a flat rock. Jake slowly pushed to his feet as the slow line came into sight and he cast a grim glance at the lifeless forms draped across their saddles. "Decided to give you trouble, did they?" he grunted.

"The short one came up with another gun," Fargo said, and saw the expression of horror slide across Jake's face.

"Oh, God. Jesus, I'm sorry, Fargo. My old Remington forty-four. It was in my saddlebag."

"They must've looked inside and found it," Fargo said.

"Dammit, old friend, this is just one more reason I'm packing it in. Reflexes are gone, eye's gone and the memory's going along with everything else," Jake Carmody said. "Let's get to town. We've a lot to talk about."

2

Night fell before they reached Loggerville. When they rode into town, Jake had just enough strength left to bring the two bodies to the undertaker and visit the town doctor, who treated his head. The doc also gave Fargo an ointment for the gunshot scrape across the top of his forehead.

"We'll talk, come morning. My office, Fargo," Jake said wearily. "I got you a room at the inn."

"Much obliged. See you tomorrow, Jake," Fargo said, and rode to the Loggerville Inn, a two-story wood-frame structure. He stabled the Ovaro in the rear and settled into a sparse but neat room. He found the kitchen open and had a steak sandwich and a lager. He welcomed a good bed and an early sleep, and when morning arrived, he strolled through town as he made his way to Jake's office.

Loggerville was much as he remembered it, much like a thousand other little towns except for the number of heavy-duty mountain wagons and dead-axle drays and logging rigs. Jake was at the sheriff's office when Fargo reached it. The man looked refreshed, but age lines stayed creased into his face and he wore a small bandage over the cut on his temple.

Fargo eased himself into a chair across from Jake's desk and stretched out his long legs. "You really packing it in, Jake?"

"Thirty years is long enough. There's a new man coming, young and full of energy. Picked him out myself. But he won't be here till next month, so I'm on the job till then. Meanwhile, I've been preparing," Jake said.

"Preparing what?"

"My new business," Jake said, reached behind the desk, and drew out a sign, a square wood plaque with red letters painted on it.

JAKE CARMODY
TRAVEL ADVISOR

"What do you think?" he asked proudly.

"Don't rightly know. What's it mean?" Fargo answered.

"It means that folks come through here all the time trying to find a way to Washington Territory or to Canada. Most want to cross the mountains. They figure it's the shortest way, but all they have is a vague idea of where they want to go and more often than not they die trying to get there," Jake said. "They don't know any trails. They don't know what they're facing. Most times they don't know what they'll need to bring. Hell, they don't even know when they're doomed by the calendar."

"And you'll advise them of all this, take them under your wing and set them straight, all for a fee," Fargo said.

"That's right. I can do it all, except for one thing. I'm no trailsman and that's what most of them will need. I'm asking you to come into business with me, Fargo. You do the trailblazing and I'll do everything else. They'll be charged extra for your fee, of course, and that'll be all yours. Everything else we split down the middle."

Fargo smiled, as much at Jake's enthusiasm as at anything else. "Jake, you know I work alone, always have. I go my way, where I want and when I want. I'm not going into business. That's not for me."

"You will be working alone, doing what you do better than anyone else. That's all you'll have to do," Jake said.

"Here, in these mountains, in this part of the territory where you've set up shop. Sorry, Jake, not for me," Fargo said. "Set yourself up as an outfitter and adviser. You'll do all right, I'd guess."

"I wanted to offer them something others couldn't, the best trailsman in the West," Jake grumbled.

"Sorry, old friend. Try getting hold of Sam Tinsley. He's a good man. He was in Kansas, last I heard."

Jake Carmody's cheeks puffed out as he blew a deep, long sigh. "I was afraid you might turn me down."

"But you had me come anyway." Fargo chuckled.

"There's always hope," Jake said. "Besides, I had another reason." Fargo's brows lifted and the older man leaned forward. "I've got a client already, maybe two. I've a man real eager to cross the Cabinet Range to reach Colfax in Washington Territory."

"That's a damn hard way to reach there," Fargo said. "But then there's no easy way from here."

"He's paid real good money in advance for a trailsman, three hundred dollars. I figure if you won't go into business with me, I can at least hire you to do a job for me," Jake said.

"I've no trouble with that, old friend. Especially with a good payroll such as that. Where is this eager man?"

"He's due here today or tomorrow. Four wagons, he told me," Jake said. "He says he's got some kind of deadline for a very valuable cargo. And a woman came to see me. She's going to Washington Territory, too. She'll pay another hundred dollars."

"Good," Fargo said.

"She'll be stopping by. I told her I expected you here this morning," Jake said, and he'd just finished the sentence when the office door opened.

Fargo looked up and saw an already familiar young woman step in, snappingly bright blue eyes, dark-brown hair swept back in a bun, and a high-buttoned white blouse. She stopped, stared at him, and her eyes found Jake.

"Come in, Miss Johnson," Jake said as he rose.

"Is this your man? Your trailsman?" she hissed.

"That's him. Skye Fargo, best trailsman in the whole damn West," Jake said.

"You mean the rudest, rottenest, most unhelpful man in the West, Sheriff," the young woman snapped.

Fargo smiled at the astonishment that had seized Jake Carmody's face. "We've met," he said blandly. "But I didn't get the young lady's name."

"Janet Johnson," Jake said.

Fargo watched the young woman's eyes glare at Jake. "If this is an example of your advice, Sheriff, I'll not be taking any more of it," she said.

"Now, hold on, Miss Johnson. No sense in making a mistake just because of some misunderstanding you and Fargo may have had," Jake said placatingly. The effort was a wasted one as Janet Johnson's reply was covered with ice.

"There was no misunderstanding, and I'll be making my own decisions now, thank you," she said.

"Now, you don't want to hire Ben Berton, Miss Johnson," Jake said.

"It seems he's the only other trailsman in town, and compared to your choice, he's a gentleman and a scholar," she said, whirled, and slammed the office door shut as she stormed out.

"I think you just lost a client, Jake," Fargo remarked.

"Jesus, what was that all about?" Jake frowned.

"We had a sort-of disagreement," Fargo said.

"Such as?" Jake asked, and Fargo shrugged and recounted what had happened.

"No wonder she's all steamed up," Jake commented when Fargo finished.

"I'm not too happy with her, either," Fargo said. "She really hooked up with Ben Berton?"

" 'Fraid so," Jake said.

24

"Berton's no trailsman." Fargo frowned.

"Berton's whatever will make him a fast buck. You know him. She arrived a few days ago and put out word she needed a trailsman. Berton went to her and told her he was one. That's when I took her aside and told her I'd get the very best trailsman for her," Jake said. "Now she'll be going back to Berton, of course."

Fargo grimaced. He knew Ben Berton. He'd seen the man in a dozen different places. Berton was as smooth as he was vicious, a back-shooter and a con man. Some of his victims were just left penniless. They were the lucky ones. The others were more often than not found dead. "You know what he'll do with her, Jake," Fargo said. "Take her money, take her into the mountains, and strand her, if she's lucky."

"Probably," Jake agreed.

"But maybe Berton's not the only one telling stories," Fargo said. "She tell you about a valuable cargo?"

"She mentioned it," the sheriff said.

"I looked inside her Owensboro. All I saw were traveling bags and hatboxes," Fargo said.

"Strange. She's stayed out of town with her wagon except for her few visits to find a trailsman," Jake said. "Maybe she's running her own game. Maybe she and Berton deserve each other."

Fargo's face wrinkled as he thought about the girl's quick fury. "Maybe she's giving out a story about valuable cargo, but she doesn't deserve Berton. Nobody does."

" 'Fraid that's out of my hands now, Fargo. Yours, too," Jake said, and Fargo nodded even as he found himself unwilling to accept the fact.

The sound of wagons pulling to a halt outside pushed aside further thoughts of Janet Johnson and he followed Jake through the doorway. Four wagons had come to a halt in front of the office, the first a platform-spring converted grocery-store wagon with a window cut in each side and curtains in place. The three were heavy dead-axle drays, each with a cargo concealed under tightly wrapped canvas and each drawn by a team of heavy-legged horses with percheron blood in them.

Eight riders accompanied the wagons, Fargo saw, all men with the tight-lipped look of hired gunmen. A man stepped from the platform-spring grocery wagon; he was of medium height, middle-aged with a round face, a receding hairline, and rimless eyeglasses, and had a slight paunch. "Hello, Sheriff." The man smiled.

"Howard Galvin," Jake said as he shook hands and gestured to Fargo.

"Skye Fargo, the Trailsman," Fargo said, and Howard Galvin's eyes lighted with pleasure.

"Then everybody's here. Good. That means we can be on our way tomorrow. I want to give the horses a day's rest," Galvin said. "Anyone else joining the train?"

Jake shot a quick glance at Fargo. "Doesn't look like it, but I'll know by morning," he said.

"Doesn't matter to me," Howard Galvin said, and gestured to the eight riders. "Insurance, in case we run into trouble."

"It's always good to be prepared," Fargo commented. His eyes were drawn to the converted grocery wagon as a woman stepped from it. He took in a bottle blond, tight curls over a round face that let too much makeup try to obscure some thirty-five or so years, he guessed. A tight dress clung to a rounded figure with at least ten pounds too much on it, high breasts made higher by the cut of a green dress, and a tight, very round rear. She wasn't an unattractive woman now, but once she must have been a hot and pouty little tease, he imagined. That was still very much in her slow glance.

"My assistant, gentlemen. Lottie Dill," Howard Galvin introduced.

Lottie's smile held the echo of her coquette years, and her eyes lingered on Fargo. "Glad to meet you all," she said with a self-made drawl.

Fargo nodded back and stepped to the nearest of the heavy dead-axle drays. "What are you carrying?" he asked Galvin.

"I'm afraid that's going to have to remain confidential, Fargo," Howard Galvin said. "I told Sheriff Carmody that it'd be a very valuable and very heavy cargo, and now you've three heavy wagons to deal with. What's in them shouldn't be of concern."

Fargo half-shrugged. "You'd best know one thing, mister. On a long, hard trip like this one anything can happen. That cargo of yours might not stay secret."

"We'll deal with that when the time comes," Howard Galvin said, and Fargo's gaze went to the riders again. Eight, plus a driver on each wagon with a shotgun on the seat beside him. Eleven in all. Was Howard Galvin simply a man who believed in being prepared for any eventuality, or was he expecting trouble? Fargo let the thought hang in his mind for a moment before setting it aside.

"There's a nice spot at the end of town where you can set up your wagons for the night," Jake put in.

Galvin motioned to his drivers and climbed onto the seat of the grocery wagon. Lottie Dill pulled herself up alongside him and showed a calf that could've been on the leg of a twenty-year-old. She tossed Fargo another slow smile as Galvin led the heavy wagons forward.

Fargo watched the procession move on and turned to Jake. "Where'd you get him?" he asked.

"He came here two months ago asking whether it was possible to cut through the Cabinet Range into Washington Territory. I told him only one man could get him through. That's when he hired me on as his adviser and said he'd be back ready to go at this time. I didn't know about the woman or that he'd be so secretive about his cargo," Jake answered.

"That's no matter for now," Fargo said. "I'll stop by later and go over things again with you." Jake nodded and Fargo strolled away. The Ovaro following, he sauntered through town and had almost reached the inn when he saw Janet Johnson talking to two men outside the general store. He paused as he reached her. "Glad to see you've taken the sheriff's advice," he said.

"Meaning what?" she returned icily.

"You're talking to others beside that con artist Berton," Fargo said.

"These happen to be Ben Berton's assistants," she said.

"No shit," Fargo grunted, and turned a hard glance at the two men. Both were young, but meanness was already in their faces. "Assistants for what? Spreading steer shit?" he remarked.

"Go get Ben," one of the men said, a light mustache on his lip. The other one scurried away.

"You're uncouth, too," Janet Johnson accused Fargo.

He grimaced. She needed help and there wasn't any polite or easy way to make her see it. "Sometimes it helps make a point," he said.

"Not with me," she sniffed.

He swore inwardly. The deeper she got into Ben Berton's clutches, the harder it'd be to help her at all. He met her disdainful eyes with a casual smile. "You're in trouble, honey, and too ornery or too damn dumb to know it," he said.

He turned at the sound of hurrying footsteps and saw Ben Berton approaching, the younger man following at his heels. Berton was tall, with a sharp-featured face and a dark handsomeness that disarmed most of the people he chose to victimize. Fargo saw the anger in the man's eyes, which he masked with a sneer. "Well, now, Mister Trailsman himself," Berton said.

"In person." Fargo smiled and cast a glance at Janet. She looked with some surprise from him to Berton. "Ben and I have rubbed shoulders over the years," he said. "I try to wash up as soon after as I can."

Berton's eyes grew harder. "Joey, here, tells me

you've been bad-mouthing me, Fargo. I don't like that, especially to a nice young lady like this," he said.

Fargo kept his voice almost amiable. "You call a jackal a jackal. That's not bad-mouthing. That's only the truth."

"I'm warning you, Fargo," Berton said in his best menacing tone. The man wouldn't draw on him, not face to face, Fargo knew. Berton knew better than to try that. "What are you sticking your nose into my business for, Fargo?" Berton growled.

"Matter of pride," Fargo said.

"What the hell's that supposed to mean?" Berton snapped.

"A man's got to have pride in his work. A trailsman is a fine, respected profession. The only trail you ever blazed was to a saloon," Fargo said, and saw the man's lips thin and his right hand twitch. But Berton kept it from doing any more than that.

"Nobody talks to me that way, Fargo," Berton growled, and Fargo threw him a sneer.

"There's always a first time," Fargo said, and saw Berton's jaw muscles pulsating. Berton was at the edge of his short-fuse temper. Only his natural cowardice and sense of self-preservation kept him from exploding. Fargo knew he had to push Berton over the edge, and the only way to do it was to give him the opportunity he couldn't turn down. It was a deadly game he was playing, he realized, where split seconds would spell the difference between life and death.

He glanced at Janet Johnson. A furrow creased her smooth brow as she watched. She'd see, he hoped, but he couldn't be sure. "Forget this creep, honey," Fargo told her. "He can only hurt you."

"Goddammit, Fargo, you've three seconds to get out of here," Berton cut in.

"He's nothing but a damn liar," Fargo said to the young woman before fastening his eyes on Berton. "I'll walk, but I'm not finished with you, Berton," he said, and turned away. He saw the glitter in Ben

Berton's eyes, which spelled only one thing. He began to walk, the muscles of his right hand tensed and his wild-creature hearing tuned to its highest. He had taken a few more than six steps when he heard the faint, sussurant sound, fabric brushing against leather, a shirt sleeve sliding along a holster.

Fargo spun, the Colt clear of its holster before he was fully turned, and he was firing, the motion fluid and swift as a ballet dancer's whirl. Ben Berton pitched to the ground, face-forward, as the two bullets slammed through his chest and Fargo heard Janet Johnson's short, gasped scream. The barrel of his Colt was already aimed at the two younger men, and Fargo saw the fear drain their faces of color as they moved backward.

"Hold it, mister. We're just hired help. We weren't going to draw on you," the one with the light mustache said, his hands half-raised.

"Get your horses and keep riding," Fargo growled, and both turned and ran, knocking into each other as they did. He holstered the Colt when they raced their horses down Main Street and peered down at Berton. The gun was still in the man's hands, he saw. He glanced up to see Jake approaching at a half-run. He turned his eyes on Janet as she looked away from the inert form on the ground to stare at him, the shock still in her face. "He drew on me. You saw him," Fargo said.

She blinked, shock still in her face. "I saw his hand move toward his holster. I don't know what he was going to do," she said.

"He was going to back-shoot me. He's made a career of that," Fargo said, and Janet Johnson swallowed as she stared at him.

"Damn you, Fargo. First you refuse to help me and now you kill the only man who came forward to help me," she said.

Jake's voice cut in. "He did you a favor, girl," he said, and she glanced at the sheriff as she took in his words. "The other wagons have arrived. They'll be leaving in the morning. You can go along. It's your decision," Jake said.

"Do I have any other choice now?" Janet returned, a note of anger and despair in her voice.

"You can forget the whole idea and go back wherever you came from," Jake said. "Maybe that'd be your best move."

Her face stiffened at once. "No," she said.

"Will we see you in the morning?" Jake asked.

"Yes," she said, the word coming from her lovely lips with some difficulty.

"With that valuable collection of hatboxes and bags?" he put in.

"That's right," she said, and strode to a gray mare standing nearby.

"You've an extra horse," Fargo commented. "Didn't notice it at the wagon yesterday."

"That's your problem," she said.

"I'd have noticed. It wasn't there."

"Maybe you were too busy repairing your bruised feelings to notice," she snapped as she climbed onto the mare.

"That how you see it?"

"Exactly," Janet Johnson said.

"I see it as a kind of lesson."

"In what?"

"In manners. In being a lady," Fargo said. "A gentleman says no, a lady doesn't run off with his clothes."

"A gentleman wouldn't say no," she tossed back, and rode away in a fast canter.

Fargo exchanged glances with Jake.

"She's another hundred dollars in your pocket. Think of it that way," Jake said.

"I've the feeling I'll be earning every cent of that hundred," Fargo grunted.

"I'll have this mess taken care of," Jake said with a nod to Berton's body.

Fargo walked to the Ovaro. "I'll stop by later," he said as he climbed onto the horse and rode from town. He turned north, then west, and slowed when he reached the baseline of the towering mountains. He rode slowly as his eyes rose up to scan the dark-green fastness. Forbidding . . . glowering . . . malevolent— the words all fit, he reflected. Like a giant beast, the mountains waited to devour those who dared to challenge their wild sanctuary. The mountains could kill in so many ways, Fargo knew: with their sudden, fierce winds, which swooped down steep slopes with the force of a stampede; with their terrible storms, which turned the earth into mud slides to bury everything in its way; with their deceptive lushness, which could hide a pack of wolves or a sinkhole big enough to swallow an entire wagon. And, of course, with their rugged, unyielding terrain, which remained beautiful even as it broke the backs and the spirits of man and horse.

And then there were the mountain people, pockets of isolated communities as much animal as man, who preyed on the unwary intruders. And last, but certainly not least, the northern Shoshoni, who called the mountains their own. With all that, Fargo found himself still wondering if he might not have more trouble from within than without as he thought about Howard Galvin's secret cargo and his band of guards. The heavy dead-axle drays would give him problems in other ways, too, and his eyes narrowed as he scanned the towering terrain in front of him. The wagons could take the strain of the land, but even the most powerful horses couldn't pull their weight up really steep paths. He'd see that Galvin was prepared for what they well might have to do, Fargo reminded himself, all preparations in place before they rolled one inch.

He moved on and spotted a distant cut into the low hills. It would serve as a starting place, an entry into the untamed, where the only things certain were sweat and exhaustion. He turned the Ovaro around as the day's shadows lengthened, and rode back to town to finally draw up before the sheriff's office.

"Good news," Jake called out in greeting. "Got another wagon for the trip. Nice, elderly couple, Jud and Irene Boxley, both pushing seventy, I'd say. One big old farm wagon outfitted with a canvas top and box frame. They're not paying the fancy money Galvin or the girl are, but it's a little more to add to the pot."

"What's bringing an old couple like that on a killer trip across the mountains?" Fargo asked.

Jake shrugged. "Thought you'd like to ask that for yourself, come morning," he said. "But they're not going to be any trouble, that's for sure." He thrust a roll of bills at the big man. "Here you are, everything paid in advance, including Janet Johnson's. She stopped by with it," he said. "It's a big-pay trip for you, Fargo. Look at it that way."

"Sometimes big pay means big trouble," Fargo said.

"Good luck," Jake said. "I won't be there in the morning. I told everyone you'd meet them just north of town where Galvin's camped now."

"Get a new partner for yourself, Jake." Fargo waved back as he rode off and the night descended. He ate at the inn and hurried to the room to enjoy the last night on a soft bed he'd have for some while. He fell asleep quickly and rose, washed, and dressed when morning broke over the land. He rode slowly through the waking town and saw Howard Galvin's wagons lined up ready to roll, the guards and drivers finishing a pot of coffee. Behind them he saw the farm wagon fitted with the canvas top.

The man and woman beside the wagon came forward as he dismounted. "Jud Boxley," the man said, and Fargo took in a trim figure, gray hair, and a lean face that matched the body, a crinkly smile creasing the lean features. The woman beside him was equally lean and trim, tall, and clothed in a simple cotton

33

dress, her face showing her age but her smile a sweet welcome. She could be everybody's favorite aunt, he decided.

"You're Fargo," she said. "The sheriff told us we'd know you by that Ovaro. He didn't tell us how handsome you are."

"Jake wouldn't admit that," Fargo said.

"I'm Irene Boxley," the woman said. "It's a real pleasure to meet you."

Fargo immediately recognized the sincere sweetness in the woman's words. He swept her husband into his glance. "Tell me, what brings two such nice folks as you heading across these mountains?" he asked.

Jud Boxley's smile was understanding. "You mean, what are two people our age doing out here?" he said, and Fargo found himself smiling in admission. "A last fling, you could say, young feller," Boxley said. "Irene and me, we raised a family, kept a nice farm with hogs and cows. Traveled across the plains and had enough hard times when we were young. But we've no children with us now. Everyone's gone their way and we've stayed on one parcel of land for too many years. We decided we wanted to have one last adventure to remember by the fire."

"That's right, a last storehouse of fresh memories before we get too old to collect any more," Irene Boxley added with another sweet smile.

Fargo admired them. They were an independent old duo. "You could be getting the kind of memories you don't want," he warned, but Jud and Irene Boxley shrugged.

"We've lived. Nothing's going to hurt us anymore, young man," the woman said, and with a nod Fargo moved on to where Lottie Dill waited on the seat of the grocery wagon. She had changed to a white blouse and black skirt that were only a shade less tight than the dress she'd worn yesterday.

Howard Galvin poked his head out through an opening behind the driver's seat. "We're ready to roll. Time's important, Fargo," he said. "What's the delay?"

"One more wagon, coming now," Fargo said as he saw the Owensboro Texas wagon approaching. "Tell your men to mount up." He waited as Janet Johnson pulled up past Galvin's wagon and came to a halt, looking coolly attractive but with another white blouse buttoned to the neck, her brown hair still worn in a bun. She offered an unsmiling nod as she swung from the wagon. "You can all meet one another when we stop to rest," Fargo said. "I'm ready to move."

Janet went to the rear of the wagon, spoke to someone inside, and Fargo felt the furrow dig into his forehead as two figures hopped from the wagon to face him. He stared down at two little girls, both wearing identical, formless, tentlike blue denim dresses and tight bonnets around their heads. White knee socks and brown leather shoes completed their attire. Ten or twelve years old, he guessed. It was hard to tell under the tentlike formless dresses and tight bonnets, though they were tall for their age, almost Janet's height. Round-cheeked faces looked back at him from inside the bonnets, not identical but close enough to be sisters, each with a small, snub nose, blue eyes, and slightly petulant lips. Tiny strands of blond hair poked out from the edges of each bonnet.

"This is Ginny Simons," Janet introduced, touching the little girl at the left. "And this is Gwen Simons."

"Where the hell were they the other morning?" Fargo snapped.

"Hidden in the trees. I didn't know who I might be bringing back to fix the wagon. I thought it best they stay out of sight," she said.

"This is your valuable cargo," Fargo said, and she nodded. "How old are they?" he asked.

"Ginny is eleven. Gwen is twelve," Janet said.

"And just why in hell are you dragging two little girls across the mountains?" Fargo shot at her.

"They are going to live in the mission school outside of Colfax," Janet Johnson said.

"You could take them down around the bottom of the mountains, along the Snake River plains, and up through Oregon Territory. It'd be a hell of a lot easier," Fargo said.

"And months and months longer," Janet said. She was right about that, he admitted silently. "They must be at the mission school by the end of the month to be admitted. This is the only way to get them there in time."

"Hell, they might never make the school this way." Fargo frowned.

"Can you guarantee they'd make it the other way, traveling months longer?" she countered.

"You know better. But on balance, it'd still be the safer way."

"It's out of the question now," Janet said.

"Who picked you to take them on this trip?" Fargo questioned.

"Their father."

"Why didn't he take them?" Fargo pressed.

"He had to go away on important business and couldn't do it," Janet answered.

"Why didn't he send some help along with you, then?"

"I was the only one available," Janet said.

Fargo tabled the answers with less than satisfaction as Howard Galvin came out and introduced himself and Lottie. The Boxleys had walked over and greeted Janet with the warmth of eternal grandparents.

"You need any help with the girls, you just call on us, my dear," Irene Boxley told Janet.

"I'll remember that," Janet said with more politeness than interest, Fargo noted, and his glance went to the two little girls. They had stayed motionless, listening and watching, their round faces under the bonnets expressionless.

"You can take lead wagon for now," Fargo told

Janet, and watched with surprise as the two little girls clambered onto the driver's seat and took the reins of the team.

"They can handle it. I taught them along the way," Janet said as she strode to the rear of the wagon and returned on the gray mare.

Fargo brought his attention to Howard Galvin. "Send one of your men to the general store in town," he said. "Have him buy an ax for every man in your party and a couple extra."

"An ax for each man?" Galvin frowned. "Why?"

"Just in case," Fargo said, and Galvin frowned again and decided he'd get no better answer, and hurried to one of the men beside the wagons. Fargo moved the Ovaro to the front of the line and waited until he saw the two men hurrying back with their arms filled with long-handled axes. He let them put an ax securely under the ropes on each wagon and then lifted one arm and waved it forward. "Let's roll," he called out, and saw Janet come up to him on the gray mare as he started forward.

"I'll ride along with you for a while," she said.

Fargo fastened her with raised eyebrow. "Let's get something straight right away, honey. I say what you'll do from here on, you and everybody else. You want to do something, you ask me first."

"Is that supposed to make you feel in charge?" she returned with an acid smile.

"I am in charge. It's to keep you and everybody else alive," he said.

"Really? Just how will it do that?" she pressed.

"Because I'll see things you won't see, smell things you won't smell, hear things you won't hear, and feel and know things you won't have any idea about. I won't have the time or the inclination to explain everything, and I'm not going to run a goddamn debating society," he said. "Is that clear enough?"

She let a moment go by, but her eyes were firm as

they met his. "I'd like to go over some things with you. May I ride along?" she asked.

"For now," he said as he turned northward to move along the base of the mountains.

She rode in silence for a long while and he noticed that she sat a horse well, back straight yet relaxed. The high-buttoned blouse moved gently as her modest breasts swayed. When she let her face relax, she was damned attractive, he concluded.

He reached the wide cut that led into the base hills and waved the wagons to follow. The cut rose almost at once, he saw as he peered ahead, but in a slow incline the heavy drays could easily take. The cut grew cool as the cottonwoods on both sides leaned toward one another to form a leafy half-roof. He had gone well into the hills when Janet spoke again.

"When we camp, I'll be staying a distance away from everyone else," she said, and paused as she caught his sharp glance.

"You a slow learner?" he growled, and her lips tightened.

"Is it all right if I camp away from the others when we stop for the night?" she corrected.

"Why?"

"I've gone to a lot of effort to keep Gwen and Ginny safe during this trip. There are all kinds of men who'd prey on two little girls. There are a number of rough-looking men with the Galvin wagons. I don't want any of them getting ideas," she explained.

"That the reason for those ugly outfits you've got them wearing?"

"Exactly," Janet said. "I don't want them looking at all attractive."

"You've done that, all right. They'll also die of heat in those clothes when we get higher into the mountains," Fargo said.

"I've some others exactly alike but made of cotton," she said.

"That won't make much difference," Fargo said.

"We'll manage," she said.

"As for camping apart, that'll depend on how far apart you mean," Fargo said.

"Then we'll talk again tonight," she said, and turned the gray mare back to the wagons.

Fargo rode on, his eyes peering ahead as the wide cut in the land continued to rise gently. He called a halt soon after noon and allowed an hour's rest. When they went on, the cut narrowed but stayed at a slow rise. Cottonwoods were still thick along the low hills, along with box elder and hawthorn. As they went higher, the bur oak and hackberry would appear and finally the giant ponderosa pine and Douglas fir.

When the day drew to a close, they were into the last of the low hills and he found a spot to camp where the cottonwoods grew back from the path. Janet pulled her wagon some twenty-five yards from the others, he saw. Much too far away later, but it was safe enough now and he decided to say nothing. Galvin's men camped off to themselves near the wagons and Lottie Dill invited him to share a meal with her and Galvin.

"What kind of time can we make?" Galvin asked.

"Depends on how lucky or unlucky we are," Fargo answered.

"There's an extra bonus in it if you make it a fast trip," Galvin said.

"I'll remember that," Fargo said.

One of Galvin's men came over, a medium-height figure, wiry and plainly hard-muscled.

"This is Hurd Bell," Galvin introduced. "Hurd's in charge of the men."

Fargo returned the man's nod.

"We'll need an extra hour in the morning, Mr. Galvin," Hurd said. "The hub's loose on the rear wheel of wagon three."

Galvin looked at Fargo. "This is the man running the show now, Hurd," he said.

"Make it a half-hour," Fargo said, and Hurd Bell nodded and hurried back to the others.

"Thinking about that bonus already, are you?" Galvin smiled broadly.

Fargo didn't return the smile. "Thinking about all the things we'll be meeting that'll push us back," he said, and with a nod to Lottie he walked back to the Ovaro.

He let the camp settle down before he took his bedroll and moved up the slope to settle under a low-branched cottonwood where he could see the camp-site below. Galvin's men had settled down quickly and he saw the lamplight go off in the converted grocery wagon. Janet had strung clothesline and put up wide sheets that walled off her wagon, he saw. She was plainly very determined to maintain the girls' privacy, certainly to keep away prying eyes. Or maybe it was just as much for herself.

He stretched out and found himself wondering about the story she had told him. She'd answered his questions, and yet each answer had left an unanswered edge to it. Why had they waited so long to start to get the girls to the mission school? If they had started earlier, they could have taken the longer and generally safer way around the southern end of the mountains. And why entrust two little girls to one young woman plainly inexperienced and in no way fit to take them on this kind of journey? That didn't make any damn sense, either. Her answers, he decided, had been not unlike a meal that filled the stomach yet failed to satisfy.

He turned thoughts from Janet to Howard Galvin. The man was a very definite question mark with his secret cargo and hired guards. He wasn't an eccentric. Howard Galvin was too contained, too smart for one of those. Maybe Lottie would provide some answers, Fargo pondered. He had seen the definite interest in her eyes when they first met. It was worth a try, he decided, and his gaze went to the last wagon where he saw the lantern go out.

Irene and Jud Boxley were the only ones that were

what they seemed to be—a devoted old couple with their minds set on a last gathering of memories. Not the usual venture most oldsters embarked upon, yet still admirable in its own way.

Trouble, if it followed, would come looking for Janet or Howard Galvin, he was certain. But maybe he'd be lucky and have only the wild mountains to face, Fargo thought as he closed his eyes and drew sleep around himself.

3

The morning came in hot and Fargo let Janet take lead wagon again but put the Boxleys after her. Janet drove and Fargo saw the two little girls watching him from the rear of the wagon, their round faces peering out from under their bonnets. He paused at the grocery wagon, where Lottie held the reins, her more than ample breasts rising up from the opened top buttons of a yellow blouse.

"You driving today?" he asked.

"I'm going to start. Howard's tired from yesterday. He'll take over later." She smiled. It was probably impossible for Lottie to smile without a certain thinly veiled sultriness, he decided, and he rode on along the path. Out of sight of the wagons, he explored the terrain as the path curved and narrowed but still remained negotiable for the heavy drays. It wasn't till midday that the path split into two forks. He halted, his gaze moving along the right fork. It rose sharply, over a small mountain that rose up as a green wall.

He studied the fork, explored it for a few hundred yards as it rose again in a steep incline, and when he returned to where the path split, the others were coming into sight. The left fork curved downward to move around the steep mountainside in a slow circle that went on beyond where he could see. As Janet rolled up in the lead wagon, he gestured to the left fork and heard her call out.

"What's wrong with going up over the top? It'll save most of a day. I can make it," she said.

"Nobody else could. Those drays are too heavy for their teams to pull up," he answered.

"I don't see why the rest of us should be penalized because Mr. Galvin has overweight wagons," she said stiffly.

"Because a wagon train's like a marriage. You're stuck with each other in sickness and health, good and bad. It usually works out," Fargo said.

Janet said nothing further, but her displeasure showed in the tightness of her face.

Fargo rode on as he waved the wagons down the left fork. The passage, while negotiable, grew rough with rocks that jutted up from the soil, so many that even the lighter wagons had to go slow. The day came to an end before they had gone very far and he chose a place to camp where a clearing appeared at one side of the passage. Janet drew her wagon off alone again and he let her.

Howard Galvin, exhaustion in his round face, disappeared inside the converted grocery wagon as soon as they stopped and let Lottie unhitch the team.

Fargo paused to give her a hand and she smiled gratefully. "Howard's not used to driving a wagon for so long a time," she said with protectiveness in her voice.

"He better get used to it fast," Fargo said, then added, "What is he used to doing?"

She hesitated a moment. "Desk work," she said, and disappeared into the wagon.

Fargo walked down past the three drays, the men camped alongside, and exchanged nods with Hurd Bell before returning to where he had left the Ovaro. He paused at the Boxleys' wagon; they were just finishing a plate of beans. Both looked as fresh as though they'd just risen in the morning, he noted with admiration. Tough old birds, both of them, he murmured to himself.

" 'Evening, Fargo," Irene said. "You know, I'm

43

concerned for that girl and those two children. I wish you'd talk to her, tell her to let me help her."

"I don't think she's the kind for taking advice, especially from me," Fargo said. "You'll have a chance to talk to her yourself."

"I will," the older woman said, and Fargo strolled away with a nod.

He sat down, ate some of the cold beef jerky in his saddlebag, and watched the camp begin to settle down. He caught the sound of voices raised from behind the wall of sheets Janet had put up again; he listened but couldn't make out words. Finally, the sounds died away. He took his bedroll and had just started for the dark of the slope when Lottie emerged from the wagon. She wore a dark-red dressing gown that clung to her full-figured curves.

He halted as she came toward him. "Thought you'd be asleep by now," he said. "Howard awake, too?"

"Howard's been asleep for hours," Lottie said. "I stayed up to talk to you. I want to talk to you about an extra bonus."

"For what?" Fargo asked.

"For looking after Howie if there's trouble," she said.

Fargo kept his voice casual but his lake-blue eyes peered sharply at Lottie. "You expecting trouble?" he questioned.

"Oh, no," Lottie said—too quickly, Fargo noted. "But on a trip like this you never know. You said so yourself," she explained.

"So I did," Fargo agreed.

"You see, if anything happens, Howie will be seeing to the wagons. He won't be watching out for himself. I want him protected, not the damn wagons," Lottie said.

"Very touching. Howie know about this?"

"No, he'd have a fit if he knew I were talking to you like this."

"What kind of a bonus are you talking about?" he asked, just to draw her out further.

"Well, I've some money of my own, but I was thinking of adding something else," she said, and he waited, letting her stumble over words inside herself. "Me, dammit," she said finally.

"Figured as much," Fargo said.

"Will you do it? Will you take special care of Howie if there's trouble?" Lottie asked. "You just tell me when and where."

"No deal, honey," Fargo said. "If there's trouble, nobody gets special favors. Sorry."

Lottie drew a deep sigh that strained the top of the dressing gown, and looked more rueful than disappointed. "I was afraid that would be your answer," she said, and her eyes searched his face again. She pushed herself up very straight, letting her breasts push up from the robe. "You sure?" she tried again.

"Real sure," he said, and saw the disappointment fill her round face. "You really care about Howie, don't you?" he asked, no sharpness in the remark.

"Howie's been real good to me over the years. He gave me a job when I needed one, and saw to a lot of things for me," Lottie said. "I never found a way to really pay him back. I thought this might be it." Lottie's hand came up to toy with one of the buttons on Fargo's shirt. "Does it make any sense to you? Can you understand what I'm saying?"

"I can. I think you'll find another way to pay him back," Fargo said, and she half-shrugged.

"Maybe," she said. "Thanks for listening. Maybe we can talk more some other time."

"Anytime," Fargo said, and Lottie stepped back with a small smile. Under her brassy blond exterior there was a sweetness, an honesty of the heart. But it had been there again, the echo of Galvin's words, the allusion to trouble and then the denial that it was expected. Fargo grunted as he set his bedroll down between two hawthorns. If trouble wasn't expected, it was feared. As he dropped off to sleep, he made a mental note to watch the land behind them as much as that ahead.

Morning came in with a burning sun. When Fargo walked down to the wagons, he saw the two little girls had changed into the cotton version of the same outfits. He was aware of their bright-blue eyes watching him as he took a fresh shirt from his saddlebag, pulled off the old one, and changed. They continued to watch him as he saddled the pinto, most of their faces encased in the bonnets. When Janet emerged to climb onto the driver's seat of the wagon, the two little girls scrambled up beside her. They watched everything with a bright-eyed curiosity, he noted. Perhaps that was common to ten- and twelve-year olds. He swung onto the pinto.

He drew up alongside Janet and cast one eye up at the burning orange sphere in the sky. "The least you can do is take those bonnets off them," he said to her.

"They'll be perfectly all right. If they get too hot, they can go inside the wagon. It'll be cooler there," Janet said stiffly.

"Not much," he said, and moved away to see Galvin with the reins in hand and Lottie beside him. Sleep hadn't done a lot for him: his round face was still drawn. Janet took lead wagon again, the Boxleys behind, Jud Boxley sporting a wide-brimmed straw hat and Irene an even wider-brimmed, floppy light hat. Both were wearing loose, light clothes and Fargo smiled as he rode past. Age brings experience, he realized, and he waved the wagons forward. He cantered ahead, almost a quarter-mile on, and found a flat ledge of rock that let him see the land on all sides. He swept the land behind with a slow glance, saw nothing to arouse alarm, and moved down from the ledge and rode on.

It was a little past the noon hour and they had skirted most of the small mountain when he called a halt at a place that flattened out into a small table of land. There was no shade, but a breeze blew down from a nearby slope and he gave the others time to rest and enjoy the wind, warm as it was.

When they started out again, it was Lottie who took the reins and Galvin disappeared inside the wagon. The little girls had gone into their wagon, too, he noticed as he rode on. The road rounded the baseline of the mountain and he grimaced as he saw it rise sharply. He rode back and forth over it and saw that the ground was hard and dry. The big drays could make it, but it'd be a strain and they'd have to go slow.

He waited as the others rolled into sight and motioned upward, pulled to one side, and watched the wagons go past. "Walk your wagons," he called out. "Every little bit will help."

Janet swung to the ground and held the cheek strap of the right horse as they started up the climb. Galvin's drivers walked alongside their teams and Fargo watched the big draft horses strain their powerful hindquarter muscles as they pulled their heavy loads. The steep section was mercifully short and the land leveled out in a high plain where the path disappeared and clusters of box elder dotted the ground.

He called another halt to let everyone rest and moved them on again in the light of the late afternoon. The drivers returned to their wagons and he slowed as he came alongside Janet. Her face was wet and shiny, and the entire back of her blouse was wet with perspiration. The front clung to her breasts in a provocative outline. Perhaps they weren't so modest, he observed.

But he saw the strain in her face and he slowed to ride beside her. "Unbutton the top of that blouse," he said, and she frowned back.

"I beg your pardon?" she said.

"You heard me. Unbutton that blouse and let some air get to your body."

"I'm quite capable of knowing when my body needs air, thank you."

"It seems not. Unbutton, dammit!"

"I really don't think that's any of your concern."

"Wrong," he bit out.

"I'm touched. Concern over my welfare. How unexpected."

"Wrong again, honey," he returned. "You're going to keel over with heatstroke soon and we'll all be delayed hours getting you back on your feet again, and that concerns me."

Her eyes flared at him. "Excuse me. I should've known it wasn't personal."

"Unbutton the damn blouse or I'll come back and do it for you," he said, and put the pinto into a canter. He wasn't certain, but he thought he heard a giggle from inside the wagon as he rode off.

The box-elder-studded plain went on for at least another five miles, he guessed, and dusk began to sift itself down over the land before they reached the end of it. He waited for the others to come along and motioned to form a half-circle amid the trees. He watched Galvin's drivers wheel their wagons into a three-sided box and saw Lottie wipe perspiration from her face as she slid to the ground and began to unhitch the team. Her skirt and blouse clung to her to reveal every ample curve and every extra pound. He moved to Janet and saw the top buttons of the blouse were unbuttoned and the flushed shininess had left her face.

"Proof you can use some common sense," he commented.

"I wouldn't want to be responsible for delaying us," she said tartly.

"Good." He nodded. "You look like you belong here now."

"What did I look like before?" She frowned.

"Some misplaced prude," he answered, and moved on without waiting for her to reply. He watched her set up at the very edge of the trees and decided to go along with her again. He had seen none of the danger signs he'd watched for so far, and he was beginning to hope that perhaps Lady Luck was going to smile on the trip. He ate alone, bedded down in a distant cluster of trees, and slept at once.

The new day came with another burning sun and he returned to where the others were camped, and smiled. Janet had the top buttons of a fresh blouse open.

" 'Morning, Fargo," Irene Boxley called out, and offered him a tin mug of coffee, which he took with a nod of appreciation. He sipped the brew as the others prepared to roll.

Howard Galvin looked only slightly less drawn as he sat with reins in hand, Lottie beside him.

"Why don't you have one of your riders drive today, Howard?" Fargo suggested.

"No. I want them where they are, alongside the wagons. I'll be fine, especially with Lottie here helping out," the man said.

Fargo shrugged and wondered how long Lottie would hold out doing most of the driving. He finished the coffee, returned the mug to Irene, and waited for her to clean up things before he moved the wagons forward. The tree-dotted plain ended another two miles on and became a wide series of rolling hills topped by long ridge lines. A half-dozen deer and moose trails spread out across the hills and he saw that none was wide enough for the heavy drays to move on without their wheels rolling along the edges. He chose a moose trail where the sides were mostly new young shoots and saplings and the lighter wagons followed him first.

He watched the heavy drays as their wheels crushed the growths along the sides of the trail with no problems, and rode on ahead. He followed trails that wandered into one another and traced an erratic path across the steadily rising hillsides. But his eyes swept each ridge now as he saw unshod pony prints, some moving along the trails, others crossing them to vanish into the bur oaks. Small parties mostly, he noted, but he counted one with at least a dozen or more riders. His jaw had grown increasingly tight as the prints continued to appear, too many of them fresh, but he'd seen nothing except the hoofmarks until he reined up at a spot where the trail leveled off and became a small table of land. He spotted an object on the ground, swung from the saddle, and picked up a leather pouch. He sat down on the stump of a tree. It was a good spot to rest and he examined his find as the wagons finally rolled up.

The pouch was a good one, fashioned of softened buckskin, carefully stitched with gut sinew, and embroidered with beadwork—the pouch of a chief or an important warrior. His lips pulled back in distaste. His hopes for just roving parties of bucks hunting deer were dashed.

Janet's wagon pulled a dozen yards ahead and the Boxleys' halted opposite him. Both Jud and Irene were down from the wagon instantly, their eyes wide as they stared at the pouch. "You just find that, Fargo?" Jud asked, and he nodded. "Then we're in Indian country now," Boxley said, excitement in his voice.

"Have been for some time," Fargo said.

Irene ran her fingers along the soft buckskin and Fargo saw her eyes were wide with excitement, too. They seemed like children beside themselves with awe and wonder. "Can you tell the tribe from it?" Irene asked.

"Northern Shoshoni," Fargo said, and Irene's spare, lean figure straightened up as she turned to her husband.

"You hear that, Jud? Northern Shoshoni, Fargo says," she echoed.

"Are we in danger of an attack?" Howard Galvin's voice cut in.

"You can never tell with Indians," Fargo said, and saw Janet listening, the two bonneted heads beside her.

"Maybe they won't see us," Lottie offered.

Fargo made a wry sound. "They've done that already, count on it," he said.

"Do we just go on or prepare for trouble?" Galvin asked.

"We move on. We can't just sit here waiting. They've seen this is no wagon train full of settlers. They might just let us go our way," Fargo answered.

"You mean without attacking, without coming into the open?" Irene Boxley said, and there was almost disappointment in her voice.

"That's right." Fargo smiled. "This is one of the adventures you don't want for your memory book." He tossed the pouch away and climbed onto the Ovaro. He let the wagons rest for another half-hour and then moved them forward. He rode not more than some fifty yards ahead and his eyes swept the terrain, picking out places to make a stand if it became necessary. He had gone on for perhaps another hour when two figures appeared on the top of a low ridge to his left, near-naked, bronzed forms on their sturdy, short-legged ponies. Fargo reined to a halt, and as he did so, a third rider appeared a dozen feet from the first two.

His eyes were moving along the ridge when the fourth horseman appeared, and now he glanced back at the wagons, which were nearing him. "Keep moving," he called out with a wave of his arm. "Slow and steady."

One of the Indians carried a lance decorated with strings of rawhide that waved in the breeze, dyed in the deep earth colors the northern Shoshoni favored. The red men appeared to be content to watch, he saw, though that could change with frightening suddenness. But he'd do nothing to cause that, he grunted as he continued to move the Ovaro forward at a walk. These four were not alone, he was certain, and he had gone perhaps another few hundred yards when he almost jumped out of the saddle. The tense silence exploded, shattered by two shots that reverberated from the hillsides.

"Jesus," he gasped as he saw two of the Shoshoni topple from their ponies while the third whirled to stare at his fallen companions. He had but a second to stare in surprise when a third shot rang out and the third Indian pitched sideways from his mount. Fargo, his jaw dropping open, spun in the saddle to stare back at the wagons. Jud and Irene Boxley were standing on the driver's platform of their wagon, each with a .44 long-barreled Henry in hand. Irene was just lowering her rifle as he heard Jud shout in glee.

"I got two of them, Irene," the man proclaimed.

"I got mine," Irene replied with a triumphant laugh.

Fargo, towering shock flooding through him, sent the pinto racing back to the wagons. "What the hell are you doing?" he shouted as he skidded to a halt beside the Boxley wagon.

"We know what we're doing," Irene said almost chidingly. "We're killing northern Shoshoni. It's what we came for."

"And we're going to get us some more," Jud said as he raised the rifle and fired again. Fargo's eyes flicked to the ridge where he saw a half-dozen bronze-skinned figures on foot pulling their slain tribesmen from the top of the ridge. Jud's shot missed this time, and Fargo, shocked horror still whirling through him, reached out and yanked the rifle from Jud Boxley's hands.

"Goddammit, no more," he shouted, spun, and saw Irene raising her Henry to fire again. He swung the stock of Jud's rifle and knocked the gun from the woman's hands.

Irene turned on him. "Now, that wasn't at all nice," she said with schoolteacher reproof.

"Goddamn, I don't believe this," Fargo bit out. "I goddamn don't believe it." He wanted to fling more words as fury replaced shock, but he held back. There was no time now for words. There was only time to find a place to make a stand, and his eyes swept the nearby terrain. A rocky outcrop jutted from a slope some hundred yards higher, a brush-covered flat ledge of land below it. The incline was steep but not too steep for the heavy wagons, and he pointed to the outcrop. "Up there," he yelled, and sent the pinto up the slope. "Fast, dammit," he called back.

He raced up to rein to a halt under the rock outcrop, which extended some twenty feet, and swept the ledge with a quick glance. The position was no fortress, but attack from the front would have to come uphill and that gave the defenders the advantage. The two ends of the ledge where the slope was less sharp were the most vulnerable, and as the big drays arrived, he ordered one wheeled across each end of the ledge as a barrier. He positioned the third dray in the center of the front of the ledge, the grocery wagon and the Boxleys' rig at either side. He ordered Janet deep under the rock outcrop.

"The girls stay in the wagon. You come up here and fight with the rest of us," he said. "You've a rifle, haven't you?"

She nodded and produced a Spencer carbine from inside the wagon. He turned and strode to the front of the ledge, where Galvin's men were already positioning themselves beneath and behind the wagons.

Galvin and Lottie, each with a rifle, crouched behind their wagon, fear more obvious in his face than hers. "Maybe they won't come after us. Maybe they'll just go away," he said, the words really a plea for hope.

"Maybe the night won't come," Fargo said, and turned to where Irene and Jud Boxley stood beside their wagon. He felt the rage churning inside him. "You stinking, lying old pack rats," he bit out. "A last adventure, storing memories for the fireplace. That was all a crock of shit, every last word of it."

"We had to come up with a reason to have you take us along," Irene said.

"Why, goddammit? What the hell are you two all about?" Fargo flung at the pair.

"The northern Shoshoni killed our two sons, their wives, and all our grandchildren in a raid. We decided to make paying them back our last mission in life. It was really a simple decision. We'd nothing else left to live for," Irene Boxley said with perfectly calm logic.

"So you were willing to sacrifice the lives of everyone else here to satisfy your damn vendetta," Fargo shot back.

"Some things can't be helped," Jud said with lofty righteousness.

Fargo stared at the couple. They were deranged, obsessed, ruled by the twisted darkness that lay inside them, beyond reaching with rational argument. Nothing mattered to them but their all-consuming hate.

"Turn them over to the Shoshoni," Hurd Bell's voice cut into his thoughts. "Maybe that'd get us off the hook."

Fargo grimaced. "If I thought it'd work, I might just go along with you," he said, and cursed at himself for the admittance. "But it won't. They're out for blood now. Besides, they wouldn't take less than three of us," he said. "Any volunteers?" he added bitterly.

"They're coming," someone called out to break the stony silence, and Fargo stepped to the edge of the center wagon to peer down the slope. At least twenty, he counted, spread out in a horizontal line on their ponies as they started up the slope. They moved slowly at first, but that would become a screaming charge when they drew closer.

"We'll take our rifles back," Jud Boxley said.

"Why not?" Fargo grunted, not without bitterness. They would need every gun they could muster, and the old codgers could shoot. They'd proved that to everyone's distress. "Over there," he said, and gestured to where he'd tossed the two Henrys. Jud and Irene hurried to the guns with spry, eager steps.

"We'll get at least four more," Fargo heard Jud say.

"Six. I won't be satisfied with less than six," Irene replied, and Fargo shook his head in disbelief. It was as though they were discussing how many muffins they'd have at the church dinner.

He returned his eyes to the hill below and saw the

line of horsemen moving steadily upward. "Don't fire till they charge," he called out, and swept the line again and halted at the figure in the center. He saw a tall, lithe near-naked torso, a strong-featured face with black hair hanging to his shoulders and shining with fish oil. The Indian wore a single white eagle's feather at the back of his head, which signified that he was a chief or a great warrior. Either way, he was the leader and Fargo put the Sharps to his shoulder and drew a bead on the Indian. Suddenly, at a signal he couldn't detect, the entire line charged, their ponies going into an instant gallop. Fargo's finger tightened on the trigger of the rifle when the Shoshoni in his sight veered sharply to the right and his shot missed. The entire line had swerved, to the right and to the left, crisscrossing one another as they charged uphill.

The volley of fire resounded from the wagons, but most of the shots missed as their targets veered from one side to the other. A second volley also missed hitting any of the attackers.

"Slow your fire. Pick one and stay with him," Fargo shouted as he saw the defenders spraying shots wildly. A Shoshoni crossed his sights and he followed it with the rifle, fired, and the man catapulted from his pony. Three arrows thudded into the wagon as he tried to find the leader again in the racing, crisscrossing figures, so he settled for another horseman. The defenders were doing a better job of shooting, he saw as he glimpsed three more attackers fall. Suddenly four Indians appeared close to the ledge at the top of the slope. He took down one and saw a volley of concentrated fire bring down two more while the third raced away.

"Hold fire," he called as he saw the Shoshoni retreating fast down the slope. Halfway down, they swerved and disappeared into the thick bur oaks at the side of the hill.

"I got two, Irene," heard Jud say.

"Same here," Irene answered, and Fargo pushed to his feet and scanned the defenders.

"Anybody hurt?" he asked.

"No," Hurd Bell answered. "Think they've left?"

"Not for a damn minute," Fargo said. He saw Janet get to her feet. "See to the girls and then get back here," he said, and she hurried back to the wagon against the deep wall.

"They charge again and we'll cut them down again," Jud Boxley said with relish.

Fargo's gaze swept the slope. The Shoshoni might well charge again. Indians often relied on the charge repeated over and over until they broke through. A costly tactic, and used mostly when the attacking force was large enough to sustain heavy losses. This wasn't the case here. This band hadn't that kind of strength. They'd try something else, he was certain. If it were another charge, it'd be with some variation. He settled back and kept his eyes on the hillside below.

Minutes went by, stretched into more minutes, and there was no movement below.

"I think they sneaked away," someone said.

"They're down there," Fargo said, and silence fell over the ledge again as time continued to drag on.

"What the hell are they doing?" one of Galvin's men broke out tensely.

"Exactly what they want to do. Making you nervous," Fargo said, and the man returned to silence. Fargo guessed another ten minutes had elapsed when suddenly three horsemen charged from the trees, raced their ponies horizontally across the slope as they swerved. An instant volley of fire erupted from the ledge, shots all missing, and the three riders disappeared into the trees on the other side.

They emerged again in another sixty seconds and repeated their horizontal dash across the center of the slope. Another volley of shots from the ledge went wild and Fargo's eyes swept the others crouched on the ledge. All were concentrated on the spot halfway down the slope where the three riders had appeared twice now.

56

The realization was a sudden stab at him. "Damn," he swore, and just as he did, the trees at the top of the hill erupted with bronzed figures. On foot this time, only a few paces from the ledge, they moved with darting speed. They had stealthily climbed up through the trees that bordered the slope and now they were leaping over and around the wagons. The defenders, their concentration on the slope where they waited for the three horsemen to appear again, lost precious seconds recovering from their surprise and precious more seconds getting to their feet.

Fargo saw two of Galvin's men pinned to the ground by arrows before they had a chance to move and a third struggle to his knees only to have a knife thrust into his back. He'd no time to see more as a leaping figure came at him across the top of the dray, tomahawk in hand. Fargo got the big Sharps up in time to fire point-blank and the Indian's abdomen disappeared in a concave red hole.

Fargo dropped the rifle for the quickness of the Colt, put two bullets into another attacker who raced at him from around one of the wagons, and the Indian dropped almost at his feet. He spun in a crouch, glimpsed Galvin pushing Lottie inside the closed wagon, and flung himself sideways as an arrow grazed his shoulder from directly above. Crouching, he looked up to see two Shoshoni leaning over the edge of the rock outcrop, firing down with their bows. The Colt barked again and the one attacker's face exploded in a spray of bone and blood as he toppled over the edge of the outcrop. His body landed with a dull thud on the ledge as the second attacker pulled his head back.

But the defenders had pulled themselves together and were firing back. He saw the Shoshoni scrambling in retreat, some vaulting back over the wagons, others scurrying beneath them. He fired at one scrambling form, missed, and saw the Indian roll to safety beyond the ledge. The attack ended almost as abruptly as it

57

had begun, and Fargo straightened up and saw the others pushing to their feet.

"How many?" Fargo asked.

Hurd Bell answered. "Four of the men killed. Two wounded but nothing serious."

Fargo's eyes swept the others as Lottie emerged from the wagon. Janet leaned against a wagon wheel as she took deep breaths. Howard Galvin, his face drawn, stayed beside Lottie. The Boxleys were untouched, disappointment in their lined faces.

"I only got one," Jud said.

"Me, too," Irene echoed.

Fargo turned away and looked down at the slain Shoshoni as the last of the day began to fade over the tall peaks.

"We roll these five down the hill. The Shoshoni will come get them after dark," he said.

Three of Galvin's men helped him as he pushed the inert figures over the edge of the ledge and watched as they rolled partway down the slope like so many broken dolls.

"Will they attack by night?" Howard asked, Lottie at his side.

"No. Night attacks aren't the Shoshoni style. Nor most Indians," Fargo said. "We can all get some sleep."

"What about my men?" Hurd Bell asked.

"We'll bury them soon as we get the time and place," Fargo said.

"If we're around to do it," someone said bitterly.

Fargo shrugged and walked to where Janet had gone to the wagon. She came forward to meet him.

"They going to be too scared to sleep?" he asked.

"No. They're fine," she said, and he glimpsed the two bonneted heads peer out from below the canvas top. "I'll stay right with them," she added, and he caught a dismissal in her tone.

"Whatever," he said, and walked away from her. He went to the edge of the ledge. Dusk had already begun to spread its lavender shawl across the mountains. He scanned the land and Galvin and Lottie came to stand alongside him. He saw Jud and Irene at their wagon, preparing some cold beans. His eyes caught the sudden movement along the ridge just past the bur oaks to the right of the slope. Movement took on form, became horsemen, and he watched the Shoshoni swing from their ponies. "They're going to camp there for the night," he said, and saw almost everyone else follow his gaze.

"I'm going to try to get some sleep. I'm not hungry," Lottie said, and he saw the fearfulness still in her round face.

"Good idea for everybody," he said, and took down his own bedroll.

The others began to settle down for the night. Fargo strolled deeper under the ledge and saw that Janet had again hung up the sheets to form a fabric wall around the wagon. She stuck to her routine, he noted as he set out his bedroll and lay down.

He lay awake some as he let his thoughts wander to the morning. It was anyone's guess what the Shoshoni might decide. Another attack with another variation? Or another direct charge? That was the least likely, he told himself. They could send a rider for reinforcements and then mount an overwhelming attack. He grimaced at that thought. Or they could play the waiting game, he realized, aware that sooner or later their quarry would have to move from the ledge.

He drew a deep sigh. All those possibilities and more. Too many to prepare for. They'd have to wait and see. The one with the white eagle's feather hadn't taken part in the last attack. He'd stayed back and directed things, proof that he was the definite leader of the pack. Fargo pushed aside further musings, let his eyes close, and slept quickly in the warm night wind.

It was near dawn when he suddenly woke, eyes snapping open at once as he sat up. Something was wrong. His intuition had stabbed at him, cut through sleep, that wild-creature sixth sense that was sometimes misread but never wrong. He pushed to his feet and his eyes swept the ledge as the first pink-gray light touched the tops of the distant peaks. He walked forward, one hand on the butt of the Colt at his hip. Hurd Bell and his men were asleep on the ground, the others in their wagons. Nothing seemed out of order until he paused at the Boxleys' wagon. The canvas flap at the rear hung open.

He stepped forward and peered into the wagon. It was empty and he muttered a soft oath as he whirled.

Hurd Bell woke, sat up, and stared at him. "What is it?" the man asked.

"The Boxleys are gone," Fargo said.

"Gone where?"

"Only one place. The ridge to kill more Shoshoni," Fargo said. "I'll go after them."

"Let them go, the goddamn fools," Bell said. "They deserve whatever they get."

"That may be so, but I don't want the Shoshoni to know we've two fewer guns," Fargo said. "If I don't get back, you're on your own." He slid past the end of the big dray and began to run in a long-striding lope that covered ground while it conserved energy.

The gray tint of dawn began to push the night away as he moved through the bur oak and onto the rise that led to the ridge. The Boxleys hadn't that much of a head start and they'd be moving slower than he. He cursed as he searched the land and saw nothing that resembled two figures. He reached the ridge without seeing them, the Shoshoni camp not more than a few hundred yards away, and he dropped into a crouch as he went forward.

The dawn had come to light the land. Thick brush and a growth of hackberry covered the ridge and he stayed low, his eyes sweeping the land as he moved forward.

He was beginning to wonder if they had holed up in a heavy brush thicket and he'd missed them when a shot rang out, a single shot followed by a chorus of guttural shouts.

"Damn," Fargo swore as he ran forward until he was in sight of the Shoshoni. They were all up on their feet except one that lay on the ground. He saw the Boxleys held captive, their rifles on the ground. They had been able to get off only one shot before they were seized. But because the Shoshoni had posted no sentries, they had managed to get right up to the sleeping Indians. As he watched, he saw Irene Boxley tied to a young sapling, Jud to another close beside her. He saw the tall, lithe Indian with the white eagle's feather standing to one side as the others lined up, bows drawn. Fargo grimaced as a volley of arrows hurled into Jud and Irene Boxley.

But none had hit a vital spot, he saw, and he watched as another volley slammed into the two figures. He heard Jud Boxley groan, but once again the arrows hadn't been aimed to kill. Three protruded from Jud Boxley's groin, two from his arms, another three from his thighs. Arrows had been shot into Irene Boxley's abdomen, legs, and arms. No bad marksmanship, Fargo realized. They were going to kill the Boxleys by inches. Another flurry of feathered shafts struck both figures, entering their bellies and abdomens. Fargo drew the Colt. He couldn't stay and watch the vicious, calculated cruelty of it. To put the Boxleys out of their misery was the merciful thing to do, and he swore silently as he saw the pain in Irene Boxley's face.

They had been people obsessed, beyond reason and beyond normal human behavior. What they faced now they had almost eagerly and selfishly brought on themselves. Perhaps they didn't deserve the merciful thing. If he killed them, it could mean his own death warrant, he realized. As he turned the bitter choice in his mind, another volley of arrows struck the Boxleys and this time both cried out in pain. However, they were still alive, bleeding from a dozen different spots as they sagged against the rawhide thongs that bound them to the saplings. The Shoshoni were laughing, taking human target practice, and Fargo swore silently. Perhaps it was pointless to do anything for the Boxleys. If he were killed because of it, the others would surely be next. Even the consequences of mercy had to be weighed against other things.

But the decision suddenly became one he'd never have to make. His concentration on the scene in front of him, he didn't hear the soft footsteps until it was almost too late. He spun and saw a Shoshoni. The Indian had obviously come up from the other side of the ridge and stared at him with mutual surprise.

"Shit," Fargo spit out as he fired the Colt and the Shoshoni flew backward as though kicked by a mule. Fargo spun and fired his next two shots into Jud and Irene Boxley while the Shoshoni were still whirling in surprise.

He used the next three bullets in the Colt to bring down three of the nearest braves, and suddenly he realized that with those he'd taken down now, there weren't more than a half-dozen Shoshoni left. But the remaining ones started to race toward him and he saw the tall, lithe chieftain circle toward him from the side with a tomahawk in hand.

There was no time to reload and Fargo spun and began to race through the brush. But the Shoshoni were quick and surefooted, and they closed ground fast, he saw. He turned, swerved sharply to the right, then left, and then right again. He was about to turn again when the lithe, near-naked figure rose up in front of him, long black hair swaying, the tomahawk in his hand.

Fargo holstered the empty Colt as five of the Shoshoni came up and halted. Their chieftain had turned it into a personal fight, Fargo realized, and he almost smiled. If he survived, that would be the end of it. Tribal honor dictated that. If he survived, he muttered in grim silence as the Indian moved toward him with the tomahawk raised.

The Shoshoni executed a tentative swipe with the weapon, more as a feint than anything else, and Fargo scooted backward. He'd never have the time to reload, so he reached down to the calf holster around his leg and drew out the thin, double-edge throwing knife. He saw the Shoshoni's eyes narrow for an instant and then the Indian moved toward him again.

Fargo circled, his eyes on the Indian's arms, and he caught the twitch of muscle and ducked as a blow came in that raked his hair. He responded with a short, upward thrust of the knife, aimed at catching the Indian under the jaw, but his attacker was quick on his feet. The Shoshoni twisted away and it was Fargo's turn to use his quickness as the Indian struck with a short, sideways swipe.

Fargo felt the tomahawk graze his chest as he flung himself backward, half-stumbled, and regained his balance in time to meet the Shoshoni's charge. He got his hand up, closed it around the Indian's wrist, and held off the tomahawk's downward blow. He sent the knife in an upward arc, but the Indian caught hold of his wrist and both men faced each other locked in a struggle of strength. The lithe figure was made of bronzed steel, Fargo thought as he pressed forward. The Shoshoni hardly moved an inch. Still locked, hand to wrist, both men pressed, half-circled, and Fargo decided it was the moment to use his weight and height advantage. He took a step back, spun the Indian around twice and released his grip to let centrifugal force do the rest.

The Shoshoni flew backward, crashed into the trunk of an oak, and fell to one knee. He started to rise, but Fargo had already shifted his grip on the handle of the blade and sent the knife hurtling through the air. He heard his curse as the Shoshoni managed to dive sideways and the knife smashed into his shoulder. With a rasping cry of pain and triumph, he rose, yanked the blade free, and charged. Fargo kept his ground, calculated split seconds, and twisted away as the tomahawk crashed downward at him. He kicked out, the blow catching the Shoshoni in the ribs, and the Indian stumbled sideways. It allowed Fargo just enough time to set himself for the Indian's next charge, and once again he just managed to avoid the short-handled ax blade that whistled past his head.

The Shoshoni came at him again, this time on the balls of his feet, and Fargo felt the tomahawk graze his temple as he ducked away, the moment of sharp pain shooting through his body. The Shoshoni wouldn't miss for much longer, Fargo realized as he backtracked. He watched the Indian come after him, the glitter of anticipated triumph in the man's black eyes. Or perhaps it was just the pleasure of a certain kill. Fargo feinted to the left, but the lithe figure went with him. He feinted to the right with the same result. The Shoshoni was almost smiling now, sensing the kill was near. Fargo continued to backtrack as he fed into the Indian's confidence. Suddenly he seemed to stumble and he let himself fall back.

The Shoshoni gave a roar as he leapt forward to come down on his foe. Again, counting off split seconds, Fargo kicked out as the Indian dived down onto him, his foot smashing into the man's groin. He saw the Shoshoni's grimace of pain as, thrown off-balance, the tomahawk missed its mark and dug into the ground. Fargo's elbow came up in a hard thrust, smashing into the Indian's throat, and the man fell onto his side, gasping for breath. Fargo whirled from his back, yanked the tomahawk out of the ground, and swung an upward blow that smashed the blade of the ax into the Shoshoni's forehead. The Indian, half onto one knee, quivered as a gusher of red poured from the split across his forehead. He tried to rise fully onto his knee, quivered again, and toppled backward to stare at the sky through unseeing eyes as the blood poured down over his face.

Fargo rose and swept the five Shoshoni who stared at him. He straightened, waited, kept victory and defiance in his face as his body ached with pain. He took a step backward, away from their slain leader, and the braves moved forward to gather the still form on the ground.

Fargo turned and walked away, his back straight as he winced in pain. He heard the Shoshoni moving away as he disappeared into the trees. He paused, dropped to one knee, and fought off the waves of pain that stabbed at him. His arm and leg muscles hurt and the scrape alongside his temple gave a burning sensation, but mostly he felt drained. The Shoshoni had been the kind of quick and powerful opponent that made him use every last ounce of every muscle and every ounce of concentration.

He was moving slowly when he reached the ledge. Lottie was the first one out to meet him, wrapping her arm around his waist. "Oh, God, you're hurt," she gasped.

"It looks worse than it is," he said as she went past the heavy dray with him and he sank down to the ground.

"I'll get some water and rags," Lottie said, and hurried away as the others gathered around. He saw Janet among them, concern in her eyes as she peered at him.

"I'm still trying to decide whether you were brave or foolish," she said.

"Your call, honey," he said. "But it's over. I killed their chief. We can go on now."

"What happened to the Boxleys?" Hurd Bell asked.

"Dead," he said tonelessly as Lottie appeared with wet rags and began to clean the blood from the side of his face. She was good, her touch gentle and the cold rags soothing. When she finished, his temple hurt less and he rose to his feet, drew a deep breath, and started toward the Ovaro. "Let's pull out," he said.

"I think you should rest a few hours first," Janet said.

"Concern? Guess it's my turn to be touched," he said.

"Wrong. I just want you fit to do your best job," she returned. He smiled inwardly. She could turn tables.

"I'll rest later," he said. "We pull out." He swung onto the pinto with muscles crying out in protest, and waited till the slain men were lifted onto one of the canvas-covered drays.

"What about the Boxleys' wagon?" Hurd asked.

"Leave it. Bring the team along. We can always use extra horses," Fargo said.

Howard, with Lottie beside him, took the lead as they moved from the ledge, Janet next in line, and then the three heavy drays. When they reached the bottom of the hill, they found a place to bury the dead and Fargo stretched out on a soft blanket of bluegrass. Lottie came to sit beside him and her round face still wore concern.

"Thanks for the nursing," he said.

"Glad I could do it. I was so afraid when I heard you'd gone after the Boxleys," she told him. "Howie's been shaken by all this. I'll be driving the rest of the day."

"We won't be moving too fast." He smiled and she got to her feet with him as the burial was finished. He returned to the Ovaro and rode by Janet's rig. Two heads appeared to watch him. One waved a hand, then the other, and he returned the wave as he rode on. Moving out ahead of the wagons, he saw the high plain become a forest that climbed up a slow incline, mostly hackberry and bur oak, and he was grateful when the day drew to an end.

He led the wagons to a place large enough for everyone to pull up with plenty of room to spare. He took a mug of coffee Lottie offered to wash down the dried beef. Everyone ate quickly and silently, Janet and the girls behind the curtain of sheets she had strung up again.

Hurd Bell came to him as the camp began to settle down for the night. "The men want to shoot some rabbits or a deer tomorrow so we can have some fresh meat. Any reason not to?"

"Not now. The Shoshoni know we're here. Any others that want to find us won't need shots to do it. Let them go ahead. They'll have time to hunt. It'll be a slow pace tomorrow," Fargo said.

"Why?" Hurd asked.

"We've pretty much run out of trails. We'll be making our own now," Fargo said, and Bell walked on with a nod. Fargo took down his bedroll and began to climb up a low rise when he saw the buxom figure wrapped in a dark robe hurrying toward him.

"I want to clean that scrape again for the night," Lottie said, and he saw the rags in her hand.

She followed him to where he halted beneath a hackberry a few dozen yards on, set out his bedroll, and lay down on it. Lottie cleaned the scrape along his temple again as he lay back, her breasts pushing up over the top of the robe as she leaned forward. Again, her touch was gentle as she used the damp rags, and he lay back and enjoyed the way her breasts pushed up from the neckline of the robe.

"Howie's a lucky man," he said when she finished.

She sat back on her legs and gave a soft smile. "He has been. So have I. He's been good to me. But I told you that," she said. "You're wondering if I'm always this attentive or if I'm just trying another way to convince you to give Howie special protection."

"Bull's-eye." He laughed.

"I should be insulted," she muttered with a half-pout.

"Maybe you should be," Fargo agreed. "But it wouldn't be the first time that's been tried."

Lottie's eyes moved across his strong, chiseled face. "I guess not," she said. "You've cause to be suspicious, I'm sure. But I came because I wanted to, nothing else."

"Thanks," he said, and Lottie stared into space for a long moment.

"I'm still in a kind of shock myself," she said. "That nice old couple suddenly turning into selfish, bloodthirsty killers. I still can't get over it."

"The world is full of surprises," Fargo said. "I'm just wondering how many more I have waiting."

"I'll be driving tomorrow. Howie's exhausted from the last few days," Lottie said, ignoring Fargo's remark and rising to her feet. "Good night," she said quickly, obviously wanting to distance herself from the question.

"Thanks, again," he said, and watched her hurry away, her full rear a round shape that stretched the back of the robe. He undressed when she was gone, and stared up at the blue velvet sky, which seemed sprinkled with silver dust, as the events of the past thirty-six hours rolled through his mind. The Boxleys had been the only ones that had seemed harmless, their reasons for the trip unusual yet perfectly believable. Yet they had so completely fooled him. What of the others? He frowned. Howard Galvin with his secret cargo and special guards. Janet with her two little charges and explanations that satisfied neither reason nor logic. What could he expect of them?

He uttered a soft oath and went to sleep wrapped in apprehension.

4

Refreshed by a night's sleep, he moved the wagons out in the new morning sun and threaded his way across a slope where Douglas fir began to replace bur oak. He kept northward and the slope grew steep, the mountains beginning to rise in all their towering majesty on all sides. He paused wherever he found a spot that let him sweep the land in all directions, and he called a halt to rest the horses soon after the sun blazed down from the noon sky. He stretched out against a fallen oak and saw Janet stroll toward him, her slender figure moving with quiet grace. He smiled inwardly as he saw that her blouse was unbuttoned at the neck.

"I was going to stop by and see how you were feeling last night," she said, caution in her tone.

"What stopped you?"

"I saw that you had someone already tending to that," she said with a smile that held more than sweetness.

"You could've come. A man can't have too much comforting," he said.

"I suppose you would feel that way."

"You want to make an appointment for tonight?" he asked blandly.

"No, thank you. You seem quite your usual self," she said, and fixed him with a chilly stare. "I just hope you won't do anything else that might be bad for your well-being."

"Such as?"

"You can fill that in for yourself," she said, and walked back to her wagon.

She was a puzzle of her own in more ways than one, he mused. She'd plainly viewed Lottie's attentions to him with disapproval. And she'd implied she didn't want him to risk trouble with Howard Galvin over Lottie. All in her own self-interests, it seemed plain. Yet there had been the hint of waspishness in her tone, and that always meant personal disapproval. But then jealousy was endemic to the female species, as natural as breathing in and breathing out. Natural and, more often than not, without any real meaning. He drew a sigh as he pushed himself to his feet and climbed onto the Ovaro.

He moved the wagons on and Ginny and Gwen waved to him from the back of the Owensboro. They were beginning to be cardboard figures that popped into view only on rare occasions, and he pulled up alongside Janet as she skirted the team around a thick-trunked fir. "Isn't it about time you brought the kids out and took those sweat-box outfits off them?" he said. "You're making a prison out of the damn wagon."

"They're perfectly fine," she snapped, her face tightening at once.

"Hell they are," Fargo tossed back, and put the pinto into a trot. Three of Galvin's men took off to hunt down fresh meat. By late afternoon they returned, not with deer, but a half-dozen big white-tailed jackrabbits, more than enough to feed everyone.

Fargo called a halt early to allow time for skinning and building three makeshift spits for cooking. Two cooking fires were set under the spits, and as the others settled down to wait, Fargo rode on in the fading light of the day. The frown that had been gathering on his brow deepened as a hot wind blew in fitful gusts. His eyes swept the tall peaks and valleys that rose up on all sides of them. The hot wind blew again, sudden short gusts, and he saw the firs and hackberrys on the high peaks bend and sway in successive movement, as though they were being ruffled by a giant, unseen hand.

He turned the horse back the way he'd come, and his lips had grown tight. It was too soon to grow alarmed, but the night would cool the warm winds and the morning sun would heat them again, not unlike a kettle boiling. All the conditions were forming, he grimaced, and while he again pushed aside alarm, he couldn't dismiss apprehension. When he returned to the wagons, the rabbits had been roasted and were ready to eat. He sat down with the others as the special treat was shared. He saw Janet and he'd no need to give voice to the question that clouded his eyes.

"The girls are very tired. I'll take a plate back to them," she said, and ignored his stare. He decided not to press her further at the moment. He had other concerns on his mind and he watched her take some of the rabbit on a plate and two mugs of coffee as she prepared to return to the wagon.

"Guess you figure strong coffee is all right for twelve-year-olds," he remarked.

"Is there anything else to drink?" she returned, her brows arched.

"Water," he said.

"They've had enough water," she said, and marched away to disappear behind the sheets that cordoned off the wagon.

He rose, took his bedroll, and went deeper into the trees until he found a spot to set his things down. He slept quickly and woke with the new dawn to find the air still hot and cloying and the small, sudden gusts of wind still swirling. He returned to the others and got the wagons rolling quickly.

Howard Galvin was still sipping his mug of coffee as Lottie pulled the rig into the second spot behind Janet. Fargo rode on ahead and his eyes again swept the towering mountains, which now rose on all sides of them, thick with Douglas fir and hackberry and long stretches of low, wiry mountain brush and the deep-green of checkerberry.

A gust of hot wind struck him, longer and harder than the others, and again his eyes reached high up at the mountains and the deep valleys between their peaks. He saw the tops of the trees move, in one place and then another, the same ruffling effect as he had seen before. When another hot gust caught at him, he uttered a soft curse under his breath and spurred the Ovaro forward into a canter. He rode on, perhaps a mile, and slowed when he spotted a distant forest of firs that covered a flattened stretch between the towering peaks. More important, it was a spot the wagons could reach. He wheeled around and returned to the others at a gallop.

They halted, concern in their faces as they saw him race up.

"Trouble?" Howard Galvin asked.

"Yes, but not the kind you're thinking about," Fargo said. "We're going to be hit by a windstorm. I've been seeing the signs of it."

"Windstorm?" Galvin frowned.

"That's right, a special kind peculiar to these mountains," Fargo said. "They happen when an overflow of warm air from the valleys at the bottom of the range rises and collides with the cold air at the top of the peaks. It starts as little ripples of wind as it gathers itself. When it fully explodes, it's compressed and channeled by the chasms between the peaks and becomes a terrible force. The Indians call it the serpent wind because of the way it rushes and curves down between the mountain peaks."

"Where do we take cover? We're in the middle of chasms and funnels of land," Janet asked.

"I found a place. It'll have to do. Drive those teams

fast and hard," he said, and saw Galvin's men put the whip to the heavy draft horses. He stayed just ahead of the wagons, waved them on up the side of a slope, then another, and through a passage between two towering peaks. He saw the others glance nervously up as a gust of wind swirled down, swept over them, and blew on its way. But another came soon after and Fargo saw the high trees beginning to bend. He swore to himself and waved the wagons forward again.

Janet was making the best time. She had the best-balanced wagon. Galvin's converted grocery wagon was the lightest, but it bounced and jounced almost uncontrollably when it moved fast.

Fargo stayed ahead but kept the wagons within sight as he felt another, stronger gust of wind. The flat stretch with the firs was still a good mile away and he swore as he heard the distant, high-pitched, whining sound. The serpent wind was gathering itself in the distant reaches of the high peaks. It would take but minutes to sweep down, he knew, and he slowed to watch the driving wagons racing after him.

"Faster, dammit. Faster," he shouted, and realized they were going as fast as they could, Janet a good dozen yards ahead of the others. His eyes went to the high slopes and he saw the trees bending, no ruffles this time but as though a giant hand was sweeping across them. The serpent winds had exploded. They were sweeping down the high peaks, funneling into the chasms.

The flat stretch of land thick with firs rose up directly ahead and his glance flashed back to the high peaks. Five minutes, he knew, five minutes before the winds would reach them. He waved back at the others as he raced into the forest of hackberry and Douglas fir. He reined to a halt, wrapped the Ovaro's reins around a low branch, and motioned to Janet as she arrived.

"There, by that fir. Face north and tie the wagon to

the tree," he said. "You've rope, don't you?" She nodded as she jumped to the ground and he helped her as she used the rope to wrap the wagon to the tree trunk. "Unhitch the team. Tie them on loose rein to another tree."

The others had rolled into the forest, saw what he'd had Janet do, and began to do the same. Fargo saw Ginny and Gwen peer from the rear of their wagon, blue eyes round.

A long, whistling sound began to fill the air, distant at first, then almost instantly close at hand. "Pick a tree. Lay facedown against the base of it," Fargo ordered. "Stay away from the wagons." He glimpsed Janet and the two little girls racing to choose a tree as he stretched out at the side of a grainy-barked hackberry. He turned onto his stomach and the whistling sound was now a high-pitched, shrill noise accompanied by a wild hissing.

He heard the sounds of small branches being snapped off before the first blast of wind swept over him, and he dug his hands into the earth at the base of the tree. The wind struck in full force and he felt loose dirt and leaves and small stones slam into him, blowing over him, and felt his body being half-lifted as the invisible force tried to sweep him along. Another blast of soil, rocks, and leaves swept over him, half-buring him under debris. He heard the wind whistling, felt it shaking the very forest. A vicious blast caught at his legs and swung him around, and he hit against the tree trunk but kept himself facedown. The forest of giant firs broke up the direct, sweeping force of the giant wind, he realized gratefully. If they'd been caught in the open, they'd have been picked up bodily and flung into the air like so many balls of tumbleweed.

As his body vibrated and quivered against the clutching wind, and the hissing, shrill sound still filled the air so not even the snapping of branches could be heard, he managed to catch the heavy, thudding sound to his left. One of the wagons had gone over. He grimaced into the dirt but didn't dare raise his head. And then, with almost frightening suddenness, his body lay still, no wind whipping at him and trying to pull him with it. The screeching, hissing sound suddenly faded into the distance. The wind had moved on, losing some of its strength as it did. He slowly lifted his head and spit out a mouthful of dirt. Pushing his palms flat against the ground, he lifted the upper part of his body and realized he was covered with a blanket of soil, leaves, and small stones. He felt most of it roll from him as he pushed to his feet, but the fine, gritty soil remained inside his clothes where the wind had forced it through every opening it found. He shook himself and knew that only a good bath could clean it away.

He peered at the scene around him. He strode forward and reached down to Janet as she made struggling motions to get up. Almost completely covered with soil, she was a small earthen mound until he pulled her free. She sat up to stare at him with shock still in her eyes. "The girls," she managed to say, and pushed to her feet to run to the next tree where two dirt-covered forms lay still.

Fargo turned to the others and saw that it had been Galvin's converted grocery wagon that had gone over on its side. He glimpsed Lottie Dill sitting up, shaking dirt and leaves from herself, and clawing the blanket of crust from Howie.

Hurd Bell was on his feet and Fargo saw that one of the big drays had broken loose to smash into a nearby tree. No real damage, though, he noted: one corner splintered but the wheel all intact. The horses had all come through it and he stepped to the Ovaro and untied the reins and the horse kicked up its legs and shook forest debris from himself.

"Let them all run free," he called to Bell and the others. "Let them shake themselves down." He shot a glance at Janet and saw her herding the girls into the wagon and he halted at the overturned rig, stooped down, and examined it as Lottie and Howard came over.

"You're lucky," he said. "It just went flat over onto its side. No real damage. Not even a bent wheel."

"God, I've dirt inside my clothes, all over me," Lottie said.

"We all do," he said, glancing at her brown-smudged breasts as they rose up over the neckline of her blouse. "You'll stay that way till we find a place to bathe."

"We're alive, thank God," Galvin said.

"Because of Fargo. We'd be dead if we'd been caught in the open," Lottie said.

"We're not, and that's all that counts," Fargo said. He called Hurd and his men to right the converted grocery wagon and gave Lottie time to straighten out the inside. But finally the horses were all hitched and he swung onto the Ovaro, feeling gritty and grimy with every move.

The sun was past noon when he led the wagons out of the forest. He found a narrow valley between high-peaked crags, and when the others were fully into the passage, he rode ahead, spurred the pinto up onto higher ridges while his eyes swept the terrain. It was past the middle of the afternoon when he spotted what he had searched for: the blue sparkle that meant only one thing, sun on water. He hurried forward and came upon a mountain lake of good size set in a dishlike dip of land surrounded by hills.

The narrow valley passed below some fifty yards to the west and Fargo sent the Ovaro down the hillside. He was waiting at the bottom when the wagons rolled into sight. He held up a hand and they halted. "There's a fine lake right up that hill," he called out. "Leave the wagons here and walk up. Ladies first."

"Thank you one and all," Lottie said, and disappeared inside the wagon for a moment to emerge with a big towel.

76

"The girls and I will go last," Janet announced, and drew a frown from Fargo.

"Any reason?" he questioned.

"We might want to take more time. I don't want others waiting on us," Janet said.

Fargo nodded as his eyes narrowed. She was quick, fast with her thoughts and her answers. But something was very wrong. He grew more convinced of it every day. He'd find out, he promised himself as he swung from the Ovaro.

Lottie, with Howard following, started the climb to the lake.

"Relax. We've plenty of time before sundown," Fargo told the others, and slid down to rest against a tree trunk. He scanned the high hills that surrounded the lake, more from force of habit than from anything else, and finally Lottie came back with Howard.

"I feel human again," Lottie said, and Hurd Bell led his men up the hill.

Fargo relaxed, let his gaze linger on Janet's wagon, where she had closeted herself with Gwen and Ginny. When Hurd and the others returned, she emerged, towels over one arm, and shepherded the girls up the hill ahead of her. As she disappeared from sight, Fargo's glance again slowly surveyed the surrounding hills. He had started to turn his gaze back to the wagons when he caught the faint movement on the hill to his right. He straightened up, peered harder, and saw the movement again, brush quivering, something moving through the trees above the lake.

He was at the Ovaro in two long strides and pulled himself into the saddle. Lottie was the only one whose eyes questioned as he sent the horse up the hillside. He was halfway to the lake when he veered to the right and continued to climb in a wide circle. His eyes flicked to the spot where the brush still shook. The hill grew steep and he slowed to let the pinto pull his way upward. When Fargo reached the hill above and to the

77

right of the lake, he had circled behind the movement of the trees and brush. He rode slowly along the side of the hill, heavy with brush and Douglas fir, and suddenly he spotted the lone figure on a brown horse.

He came up behind the figure and moved closer before the man turned and saw him. Fargo took in a straggly beard and unkempt black hair sticking out from beneath the floppy brim of his torn, oversize stetson. He rode a bony nag of a horse and sported a stained shirt and patched Levi's. Fargo knew who he was at once. One of the mountain people, he muttered inwardly. Strange clusters of people who had developed an isolated life high in the mountains, entire inbred families of them, amoral, feral, with a cunning craftiness that let them survive. They were shunned even by the Shoshoni, who regarded them as some kind of evil spirits. They had been known to journey to the base of the mountains and make off with young girls belonging to some hapless settler or wagon train.

Fargo saw the man's hand rest on the stock of a big old Hawkens plains rifle he carried in a scabbard. " 'Afternoon," Fargo said and the man peered at him out of dark, hollowed eye sockets.

"Who be you?" the man growled.

"I'm just passing through," Fargo said. The man's long face reflected only suspicion and hostility. But that was probably his usual state, Fargo reckoned. "I'd take it kindly if you'd stay away from the lake," Fargo said.

"Why?" the man grunted.

"Got some friends bathing there. They wouldn't want company," Fargo said.

A crafty smile touched the long, lean face. "Must be gal folks," the man said.

"Didn't say that," Fargo answered.

"You wouldn't be asking me to stay away otherwise," the man said, and Fargo silently cursed his native cunning.

78

"Whatever." Fargo smiled. "But I'd appreciate you staying away."

"My mountains. I go wherever I want, mister," the man growled, and his hand went to the stock of the rifle. He halted and stared at the Colt, which had appeared as if by magic in Fargo's hand.

"I asked. Now I'm telling," Fargo said, his voice hardening.

"Pretty damn fast with that thing, aren't you?" the man said.

"Pretty damn on target, too," Fargo said. "Now, you just ride off north, cousin."

The man shrugged and turned his horse. He rode away at a slow walk and Fargo watched him go until he vanished into the heavy tree cover. He backed the Ovaro into the firs just behind him and waited, his eyes on the place where the man had disappeared. He let at least five minutes pass before he moved into the open, satisfied he'd have seen or heard the man had he tried returning. He started to walk the horse west and his eyes scanned the high hills when his wild-creature hearing caught the faint sound, the soft rustle of brush being pushed open and then the swish of air.

He flung himself sideways from the saddle and managed to catch a glimpse of the heavy-handled hunting knife hurtling through the air at him. It slammed into his back as he dived, but it hit the thick leather of his gun belt and fell away as he landed on the ground. He lay still, half on his side, his eyes barely slits yet enough for him to see the figure come hurrying toward him. The man had left his horse and come back on foot with silent steps, as natural to him as to a mountain lynx.

Fargo waited, let the man reach him, and as the hollowed-eye face leaned down, he exploded with a savage kick that caught the man in the knee. The man dropped to his other knee with a howl of pain, and a ripping, backhand blow smashed into his jaw. He flew backward, hit the ground heavily, and lay still. Fargo rose, picked up the hunting knife, and flung it a dozen yards into the brush.

He stepped back, waited as the man finally pulled his eyes open, took a minute to focus, and then slowly pushed to his feet. He peered at the big man in front of him and there was fear in his face now, along with a trickle of blood that ran down from one corner of his mouth.

"You come back again and it'll be your last trip anywhere," Fargo growled, and the man nodded, relief mixing with the fear in his lean face. He turned and hurried away, quick steps that took him into the trees in moments. He wouldn't return, Fargo was satisfied. The fear in his face had been real. Nonetheless, Fargo let another five minutes pass, his eyes riveted on the trees, before he swung onto the Ovaro and rode west.

The lake was only a few thousand yards ahead and below, and he moved the horse downward through the firs. The glint of clear blue water flashed through the trees and he continued to move downward. Janet, no doubt, had the girls dressed already and was probably finished herself. But if she wasn't, he'd enjoy the moment. The appreciation of beauty was an honorable pursuit. Besides, he may have saved her from a really unpleasant experience and he deserved a free look. Not that she'd agree, he grunted.

He reached the end of the firs that bordered the lake and halted. Janet, a towel wrapped around herself, stood near the edge of the water and he saw her clothes hung over a tall bush.

But he didn't see the girls. The furrow had just formed on his brow when the surface of the water burst upward in a spray and he saw the two forms come up with giggles and playful shouts. The furrow on his brow became a frown as Ginny and Gwen rose in water that only went to their hips. He stared in openmouthed astonishment at the two, magnificently proportioned, nubile young women, both with full, deep breasts, cream-white and tipped by light-pink nipples, round chests, narrow waists, and very womanly hips. They pushed through the water to the shore and he saw full, gorgeous thighs, slightly convex little bellies with dense, tangled black naps that glistened with drops of water.

"Goddamn," he breathed in something close to utter astonishment. "Eleven and twelve years old, my ass!"

5

Surprise and appreciation continued to leap inside him as he watched the two girls begin to dry themselves. They wriggled, twisted, used their full, opulent bodies as though they were dancing, magnificent breasts jiggling, hips undulating as they plainly reveled in being free of their encompassing outfits. He couldn't tell them apart any better with their clothes off than when they were in the formless clothes, though he noted that one had a slightly denser nap than the other. Suddenly he realized that while he'd been watching Gwen and Ginny, Janet had stepped behind the bush and reemerged dressed.

The two sisters finished drying themselves and drew on half-slips and then the formless dresses.

"Christ, I've had enough of these things," he heard one say.

"I'm not wearing these damn bonnets another day," the other said.

"Yes, you will indeed," Janet snapped, and Fargo moved the Ovaro into the open. Janet was first to spin around to see him in surprise.

"Forget the bonnets. The masquerade's over," he said.

"Hooray," one of the girls half-shouted, and gave Fargo a bright smile.

"You," Janet hissed, her snapping blue eyes narrowed at him. "You've been spying on us."

"Didn't start out that way," Fargo said.

"How rotten. How positively rotten," Janet accused.

"Almost as rotten as lying your little ass off," he returned. She glared back but her lips stayed tight. "You want to start with the truth now," he said, and glanced at Gwen and Ginny. Up close, he saw that one had slightly fuller lips and her hair was a shade darker yellow.

"A little disguise, that's all," he heard Janet say, and he brought his eyes back to her. "That's hardly such a sin," she added.

"Depends," he said.

"Everything else I told you is the same. I'm taking Gwen and Ginny to the mission school," she said.

His eyes went to the girls. "That true?"

"Yes," one said, and the other nodded agreement.

"Which one are you?" Fargo asked.

"Ginny," she said.

"How old are you, really?" he questioned.

"Nineteen," she said, and his eyes went to Gwen.

"Eighteen," she said with a certain insouciant pride. She had the fuller lips and a shade darker blond hair, he noted.

"Why the masquerade ball?" he growled at Janet.

"I thought they'd be safer if they were disguised as little girls," she said. "A decision. I don't apologize for it at all. Everything else is just as I told you." Her eyes met his without a waver and he glanced at Gwen and Ginny.

"Your father hire her to take you to the mission school?" he asked, and they nodded in unison.

"I don't appreciate having my word questioned like this," Janet put in icily.

"Tough shit, honey. I don't appreciate being tricked," he snapped back, and heard a little giggle from the girls. He shot both a piercing glance again and both shrugged. He turned away, his jaw tight. He hadn't been satisfied with Janet's story the first time. He still wasn't satisfied. Something still wasn't right, even though the girls seemed to back her up. He returned his eyes to Gwen and Ginny. "You two have any other clothes?" he asked.

"Back in the wagon," Ginny said.

"Put them on when you get back. Enough of this disguise game-playing," he said, and received wide, warm smiles from both girls.

Janet made no protest and he followed as they walked down the hillside to the wagons. Gwen and Ginny scurried into their rig and emerged in black skirts and white shirts that did nothing to hide their very mature figures. He saw the others stare in surprise.

"I'm both surprised and confused," Howard Galvin said.

"Talk to Janet. I'm going on to find a spot to bed down," Fargo said, and put the pinto into a fast trot. He stayed in the valleylike passage, and as dusk began to settle, he found a place where the land widened and a hill of ponderosa pine rose up at one side. He unsaddled the Ovaro and had just finished giving the horse a fast but thorough brushing when the others rolled to a halt.

Night descended and they all ate quickly, clean but tired, and Janet and the girls stayed to one side. Without curtains this time, and when the meal ended, Gwen and Ginny waved at him as they climbed into the wagon. As the others prepared to sleep, Fargo took his bedroll and climbed the hill to a level spot beneath the long needles of a big ponderosa.

He set out his bedroll, undressed to his BVDs, and stretched out in the warm night as his thoughts slowly turned. First the Boxleys. Now Janet and her masquerade. That left only Howard Galvin and his secret cargo. Had he another set of surprises waiting? Were none of them what they had claimed to be at the start of the trip? His thoughts broke off as he heard the rustle of brush, footsteps moving tentatively. He pushed up on one elbow, the Colt in his hand at once. He saw the moonlight outline a figure pushing through the high brush.

"Looking for somebody?" he asked softly, and saw the figure turn and hurry forward toward him. It came closer, took on features, and he saw a white shirt and black skirt, then the round snub-nosed face.

"There you are," she said as she sank to her knees on the bedroll. Full lips, he noted, the shade of her blondness impossible to tell in the moonlight.

"Gwen?" he offered, and received a warm, wide smile.

"Very good," she said, and he saw her eyes slowly and appreciatively move across the naked symmetry of his muscled body. "Wow," she breathed, and turned another smile at him.

"What are you doing up here?" Fargo asked.

"Came to see you. Ginny and I drew straws. I won."

"Janet know you're up here?"

"God, no. We told her we were sick of sleeping in the wagon and were going to take our blankets outside," Gwen said.

"And you sneaked away," Fargo said.

"After she went to sleep." Gwen giggled.

"Why?"

"We've been watching you ever since we started. Of course, we couldn't talk to you, so we wanted to thank you for everything you've done," Gwen said, and he saw her eyes move across his body again.

"That's real nice of you. Any other reason?"

Gwen allowed a tiny, seductive smile to edge her lips. "You shouldn't be suspicious, Fargo."

"I figure you could've found a way to thank me tomorrow sometime or other," he said mildly.

"We like to thank people our way," Gwen said, and he felt the surprise push at him as suddenly her lips were on his, soft and moist, and he felt the tip of her tongue dart out and quickly draw back.

"That's a real nice way of saying thanks," Fargo said as she drew back.

"That is only the beginning," Gwen said, the little smile toying with her lips again, and he saw her fingers begin to unbutton the shirt.

"This the way you always say thanks?"

"Oh, no. Just to those worth saying it to this way," Gwen said, reaching the last button.

"This a joint decision?"

"I told you, we drew straws," she said, and undid the last button. Her breasts pushed out into the open, magnificently formed, full-cupped, with light-pink tips on matching circles, twin pastel points on the cream-white skin. She shrugged and the shirt fell from her entirely, and he took in smoothly rounded shoulders and a narrow waist beneath the gorgeous breasts. She sent out waves of unvarnished sensuousness, a totally hedonistic little creature, he decided, and he felt the surging inside him. She came forward again and her mouth found his, her breasts softly exciting against his chest, the tiny pink nipples rubbing his skin with a delicious sensation. He returned her warm, moist kiss and drew back for a moment even as his loins surged far beyond ignoring.

"Something wrong?" she asked.

"Wouldn't exactly say that," he said as her hand rubbed against his chest. "I'm just wondering how much Janet hasn't told me about you two."

"We know what she told you."

"Was it a lie?"

"No, not so far as it goes," Gwen said with a touch of crypticness.

"But there's more," Fargo pressed.

The lovely breasts lifted as she gave a half-shrug. "I didn't come here to talk about Janet or anything else," she said, and her mouth was on his again, lips working, demanding.

His hand curled around one magnificent breast, his thumb rubbing across the small pink tip. Gwen gave a low, purring gasp and her tongue darted out, probed, curled, transmitted its lustful message.

"What the hell," he muttered as his mouth opened against hers and he responded to her wanting. He swung her down beside him and his lips left hers for a moment to press one firm, full breast.

"Yes, Jesus, ah, yes," Gwen murmured, and he felt her hand pushing her skirt down when a loud shout cut into the moment.

"Gwen Simons, where are you, damn you?" it called, Janet's voice sharp with frustration and fury.

"Shit," Gwen hissed as she sat up and she reached for her shirt. Fargo saw Janet whirl as she picked up the sound and marched toward them. Gwen had the blouse on but still unbuttoned as Janet reached them and halted, hands on her hips as she glared at Fargo first, then at Gwen.

"You get back to the wagon this minute, do you hear me?" she ordered. Gwen rose, one hand buttoning the blouse as she walked away with her hips swinging defiantly. Fargo met Janet's eyes, which shot blue fury at him. "I don't believe it. You were about to indulge her," she hissed.

"Indulge her? What's that mean exactly?" he asked.

"You know perfectly well what it means," Janet snapped. "She's barely a woman. How could you?"

"I'd say she's very much a woman," Fargo returned mildly.

"She's eighteen. It would be indecent. Immoral. Improper. Totally unthinkable," Janet flung at him.

"That's one way of seeing it. There are other viewpoints," he commented.

"I can't imagine any," she said, and started to turn away when she paused and fastened a searching glance at him. "I must say I'm wondering what would have happened if I hadn't come along." She frowned.

"That makes two of us, honey," Fargo said.

"I'd like to think better of you," she said.

"So would I," he said cheerfully. "But sometimes the spirit's weak. Human nature."

"Or a convenient excuse," she snapped as she strode away.

He lay back and smiled at the truth in her answer. He wondered what she'd say if she knew that Gwen had come asking to be laid? Or did she suspect as much? Was her righteous indignation real or one more part of the masquerade? He'd find out, he was becoming increasingly certain. There was the kind of heat in little Gwen that would keep burning. He turned on his side, pushed away further speculation, and let sleep envelop him.

When morning dawned, he returned to the wagons and saw Ginny and Gwen in their skirts and shirts, chattering with Howard Galvin and Hurd Bell while Janet waited with reins in hand, her face tight. Gwen saw him as he arrived and threw him a big wave, followed by another from Ginny.

He paused beside Janet. "Not even a small wave?" he asked.

"I'm not the waving kind," she sniffed.

"What kind are you, I'm wondering," he said.

"You can keep wondering," she said, and he rode on.

"Let's move," he called out. The wagons were lined up, Howard first with Lottie beside him, Janet and the girls second, and the three heavy drays last. He rode on and the valleylike tract came to an end as the land rose, dense with thick, tangled mountain brush that only a lone horse could carefully pick its way through. He let the Ovaro move up through the tangled, tentaclelike stalks, far enough to see that, far beyond where the thick brush ended, there were passes and cuts through the mountains the wagons could handle.

But first there was the sea of impenetrable, dense brush. He turned the horse around and picked a path back to the bottom of the rise. He reached it as the others rolled up and he swung to the ground, then took the Ovaro to one side where he could graze on a patch of wheatgrass. "Get those axes," he said to Hurd Bell. "Everybody takes one and starts chopping."

Janet stared at the sharply rising mountainside of tangled brush. "It'll take all day to get halfway up," she protested.

"It'll take longer if you stand around jawing about it," he said.

"Isn't there another way?" she asked.

"You see one?" he returned, and she fell silent.

Galvin's men distributed the axes and Fargo let his bite into a tangled cluster of brush in front of him. "It's not so bad. It's dry and cuts easily. Form a row and start chopping," he said, and Lottie took her place beside him. "Chop away the heavy, tangled pieces so the horses won't be tripped. The wagons can roll over the rest," he ordered, and began to swing his ax.

He set a steady pace and the others kept up, but Janet, then Lottie, and finally Gwen and Ginny fell back. He called a halt to rest and took it more slowly when they began again. The task seemed insurmountable, yet they were making progress, painfully slow as it was. By afternoon he felt the ache in his own back and arms and called another halt.

"God, it seems we've done nothing," Janet said, looking back down the hill.

"That's the way it's going to go, a little at a time," Fargo said. He set a slower pace as they began again, and called an early halt as the day began to slide toward an end. "Go down, get your blankets and food, and bring it all back," he said. "Then I want somebody to stay down and tend to the horses until we're finished."

"I'll do that," Howard Galvin volunteered quickly, and Fargo smiled inwardly. Howie knew the lesser of two evils when he saw it. But it was just as well, Fargo concluded. The man was puffing and sweating more than anyone else, and accomplishing less.

"It's yours," he said, and Galvin couldn't keep the relief from his face as he started down the hill with the others.

Hurd Bell and his men were first back with their gear, and the others followed as night came. They bedded down on the hillside, each clearing away a place of chopped brush to lie down and sleep.

Morning finally dawned and the day was a repeat of the previous one, and when it ended, they were all grateful they had their blankets on hand as they quickly fell into the deep slumber of the exhausted.

The next day brought a welcome surprise as the brush became drier and more brittle. One blow of the ax instead of three or four was enough to shatter the tangled webs of woody threads. They reached the top of the mountainside before the day ended and the land flattened to form a small table.

Fargo led the way back to the bottom where he had the heavy drays climb first so their weight would further flatten the chopped brush. He rode alongside Janet as she followed the last dray, Gwen and Ginny beside her as they tossed wide smiles his way. They seemed improperly fresh and still energetic, he noted. Youth, he growled silently.

When they reached the top, the night began to descend and they ate in silent exhaustion. Fargo waited till everyone had bedded down, then he started to carry his bedroll off to one side and saw the two, blond, full-figured forms appear.

"Thought you'd be done in by now like everyone else," he commented.

"We are," Ginny said.

"I just wanted to tell you I'm sorry about the other night," Gwen said to him.

"Sorry you came?" he asked.

"No, sorry we were interrupted," she said. "I've something to finish now."

"I think you've something more to tell me first," Fargo said.

"Maybe." She smiled, leaned forward, and pressed her lips to his. "Till next time," she said, and stepped back.

He saw Ginny move and then her mouth was on his, a softly sensuous touch. "Till whenever," she murmured, and both spun and hurried away.

He frowned in thought as he took his bedroll some twenty yards away on the table of land. Nothing was as it seemed on this caravan. Gwen and Ginny, unmasked, still wore masks, he decided as he undressed and let sleep push aside further wonderings.

When the new day came, he led the wagons through a passage between tall ponderosa pines, and when he rode on ahead, he found footprints in the soft earth. None fresh, but none made by soft-soled Indian moccasins. These were heavy, heeled bootprints. Trappers, perhaps, he considered, and his eyes swept the mountain terrain that rose up on all sides. But he saw nothing except flights of songbirds, Bullock's orioles to his right, shrikes to his left. He returned to surveying the crevices, passes, and gorges that threaded their way through the high crags. He dismissed three at once, one too steep for the wagons, another too narrow, and the third made of boulders that would snap an axle in minutes.

He finally found a cut that turned eastward and a little out of their way, but he rode into it. "Beggars can't be choosers," he muttered as he explored the cut. He spied a high flat ledge that only the Ovaro could reach, and once atop it he could see for miles in all directions. He'd taken a cursory glance back at the land they had left behind when he snapped his gaze back to the distant hills. A line of trees shook and Fargo's eyes narrowed as he followed the movement of the trees. No stray wind, the leaves moving in an isolated, straight line, he noted. Horsemen moving through the forest, traveling fast, enough of them to make the trees move. He watched the motion of the trees trace their route and felt the furrow dig into his brow. The horsemen were moving in the exact same paths the wagons had taken.

Coincidence? Fargo asked himself. Possible, he realized, yet unlikely. A band of hard-riding horsemen traveling through the mountain fastness was unusual of itself. It'd take little effort to pick up wagon tracks, and he took another glance at the distant hills before he rode back down to the cut.

Night wasn't far away. The horsemen would camp. He'd have another day to determine if they were following the wagon tracks, Fargo decided, and he said nothing to the others as they rolled up. The cut stayed narrow and as dusk began to settle he called a halt. "We camp here," he said.

"Here, right in the middle of the cut?" Janet protested.

"It doesn't widen any and I didn't find anyplace else," he told her.

"It's like camping in a tunnel. It makes me feel funny," Janet said, shuddered, and hurried to the wagon. For the first time, he'd glimpsed a crack in her facade of contained assurance.

"I just want to sleep," Howard Galvin muttered as he disappeared into his wagon.

Fargo walked past the wagons with his bedroll and set it a dozen yards up the passage. He slept quickly but restlessly and woke twice at the sound of bighorn sheep leaping along the rocky crags.

When morning came, he led the others through the long, slow circle of the cut until it finally ended and opened onto an expanse of sharp and craggy slopes. He chose one where the pines grew least thickly and the wagons had room to maneuver as they struggled upward. He waited, watched them start, and satisfied that they'd make it despite the steepness, he rode onto higher ground, found a crevice, and made his way to a crag where he could survey the terrain they had traveled.

It took him a moment, but he found the signs that marked the line of horsemen. He watched as they came into distant view, hardly more than a cluster of dark shapes moving together. But he saw them start up the steep slope of thick brush that had been chopped away, and his lips pulled back in a grimace of distaste.

The hanging question had been answered. The horsemen were following the wagon tracks. He estimated the day would be near an end before they caught up to them. He carefully made his way from the crag and returned to the steep slope, rode on farther, and found where it leveled off to become a high plain broken up by tall rock formations.

He halted and the day had moved into the afternoon before the wagons crested the steep slope and rolled to a halt. The horses needed at least an hour's rest, he saw, and he slumped down against a rock and watched the others stretch out in exhaustion.

Gwen and Ginny detached themselves from Janet and sauntered over to sit down beside him, and he caught the disapproval in Janet's eyes. "You going to find us some nice, quiet spot to camp for the night?" Gwen asked. "Janet's real tired. I think she'll sleep hard."

"I'm not sure what tonight's going to bring," Fargo said, and drew an arched eyebrow from both girls.

"Something wrong?" Ginny asked.

"Don't know. I'll talk more about it later," he said, and both gave little half-shrugs.

Gwen stretched out on her back, her full-cupped breasts rising beautifully to pull the fabric of her shirt taut. As if not to be outdone, Ginny stretched out beside her and both rested, eyes closed but tiny smiles edging their lips.

Being provocative was built into them, Fargo decided. They were damn good at it, he grunted as he saw some of the men watching them. He closed his eyes, rested, and when the hour was over, he rose and Gwen and Ginny pushed to their feet with bouncy gracefulness. After they skipped to where Janet waited at the wagon, Lottie paused at Fargo's side.

"Seems you have a real set of admirers," she said. "I saw one of them stop by to see you the other night. Maybe 'admirers' is too weak a word."

"It'll do," he said.

"You turned down an offer I made you. I guess I'm just not young enough," Lottie said, and he heard the hurt in her voice.

"You offered me a deal. That's what I turned down," he growled.

She blinked back and a little sigh escaped her. "Yes, you're right. I apologize," she said. "But thanks."

"For what?" He frowned.

"For implying that if I hadn't hung a deal on it, you wouldn't have turned me down," she said.

"Try me again." He grinned and she hurried away with gratefulness in her quick smile. He swung onto the Ovaro and waved to the others. "Stay to the right, between the two rock formations there," he said, and put the horse into a fast trot.

He rode through the tall rocks, slab-sided granite formations, emerged to find more of the same but with enough room for the wagons, and he turned to halt at a ledge that looked down at the terrain below. His eyes found the horsemen behind them but closer, and he counted some ten riders, peered again, and changed his count to eight. They were gaining ground fast now, and they'd be real close by dusk.

He rode on another hour and then let the wagons catch up at a spot where a tract of ground widened, almost surrounded by high rock. He dismounted and let the others roll up and motioned to them to camp.

When the horses were unhitched, he strolled forward. "Got a question," he asked, and drew everyone's attention at once. "We're being followed," he said. "Small posse. Some eight riders, far as I can make out. Anyone know why we're being followed?" He kept his voice casual as his eyes swept the others, slowed at Howard Galvin.

"Search me," Galvin said, and Fargo glanced at Lottie, who shrugged.

"I sure as hell don't know," Hurd Bell volunteered and Fargo's eyes paused at Janet.

"I haven't any idea," she said. "Maybe they're not following us. Maybe you're wrong."

"A posse, way up here in these mountains, following in our tracks. Hell I'm wrong," he said, and she shrugged. He grunted silently. Either she was lying or Galvin was lying. Or perhaps all of them, including Lottie. Maybe Lottie had a few skeletons in her own closet. Or perhaps one of Hurd Bell's men was wanted for something. He couldn't dismiss any possibility. But someone was lying.

He glanced at the sky where the purple of dusk had begun to gather at the edges of the high peaks. It was highly unlikely their followers would come any closer with so little light left. They'd make camp below and wait for the morning.

"What do we do?" Galvin asked, cutting into his thoughts.

"We eat and you get some sleep," Fargo said, and Galvin frowned.

"What about you?" he asked.

"After it gets dark, I'm going to pay our new friends a little visit," he said. "I'm going to find out why they've been tailing us."

"You could get your head blown off doing that, Fargo," Hurd said. "You don't know anything about those varmints."

"I'll be real careful," Fargo said.

"Maybe they're a bunch of mountain bandits who picked up our tracks and figure to make an easy killing," Bell said. "I say we hole up here, let them come up, and blast them if we have to."

"That's a good idea," Howard Galvin said.

"Yes, absolutely," Janet agreed.

Fargo smiled inwardly. Everyone seemed very eager for him not to go asking questions. "We might end up having to fight them off anyway," he said. "Meanwhile, maybe I can prevent that. I'll give it a try."

"Suit yourself," Hurd said. "But I don't take to the idea of being stuck up in the middle of these mountains without you."

"I'll keep that in mind," Fargo said, and turned away as the others prepared to eat.

Night settled down soon and everyone stayed to their wagons, he noticed, except for Bell and his men. He relaxed against a rock and let the night deepen a little further before he rose and walked to the Ovaro.

Lottie stepped from the wagon as he passed and he halted. "They're not after Howie," she said. "Whoever they are, they're not after Howie."

"What makes you so sure?" he asked.

"I just know," she said stubbornly.

"That's not enough," he said.

"It'll have to do," she answered, and slipped back into the closed wagon.

He swung onto the Ovaro and rode slowly from the circle of tall rock formations. Under a half-moon sky, he made his way downward, his eyes searching the night until he found the small orange glow of a camp fire. He threaded his way toward it, slowed, and dismounted as he drew close enough to see the figures seated around the few logs, which were beginning to burn out. Eight men, he counted again, nothing unusual about any of them, all armed with six-guns and many with rifles in their saddle packs, he noted.

"What about the others?" one of the men asked.

Another answered, "We kill them too if we have to." The man rose to pour the remains of a mug of coffee onto the fire.

Fargo took in a tall figure, black-haired, with a hard face that sported a mustache and thick eyebrows. The man wore an elkskin vest over his shirt. "We try to do it the easy way. If we can't, we do it the hard way," he told the others. He was plainly the leader.

Fargo turned the man's words in his mind. There had been nothing but icy ruthlessness in them, and he slowly, silently drew the big Sharps from its saddle holster.

He dropped to one knee, raised the rifle to his shoulder, and took aim at the man with the elkskin vest. "Hold it right there, mister," he said, and saw the man spin, start to reach for his gun. "Don't do it," Fargo said. "There's a big Sharps aimed right at your gut."

The man dropped his hand to his side. "Who are you, mister?"

"I'm the Trailsman, leading those wagons," Fargo said. "Who are you after? Why are you following us?"

"None of your damn business," the man said, and Fargo let his eyes flick to the others. They were frozen in position, bodies tensed, waiting as they peered into the trees.

"This rifle says it's my business," Fargo returned. "Who are you chasing?"

"Come out where we can see you, mister," the elkskin vest said.

"No, thanks," Fargo said. "I'm waiting for that answer." He saw the man's mustache quiver as he wrestled with his decision. "What part of your gut do you want it?" Fargo growled.

"Those two little bitches and the one that's running away with them," the man blurted, and Fargo felt the moment of surprise stab at him. He'd been wagering with himself that it'd be Howard Galvin.

"Why?" he asked.

"That's our business. You got your answer," the man said. "You want to make a fast hundred for yourself? Turn them over to us."

"Why?" Fargo repeated.

"Just turn them over. That's all you need to do," the man said.

"One more time. Why?" Fargo said, his voice hardening. His concentration on the man in his sights, he barely caught the flicker of movement from one of the men stretched out at the edge of the circle. But he was already flinging himself sideways as the shot rang out. He hit the ground as the shot became a fusillade of bullets and he rolled, stayed flattened on the ground as bullets whistled all around him.

They slowed their fire and some paused to reload. Fargo rolled and came up against the Ovaro. They were firing again, but they didn't rush into the blackness of the trees. The Trailsman rose, took hold of the Ovaro's reins, and yanked hard. The horse broke into a canter and he ran alongside the pinto until he half-leapt, half- pulled himself into the saddle. They didn't come after him, but he hadn't expected they would. He raced through the trees and slowed only when he reached the foot of the mountain. He let the Ovaro set its own pace up the steep slope and the moon was more than halfway across the blue velvet sky when he reached the campsite in the circle of a tall rock formation. He had part of his answer. He'd get the rest here and now, he muttered as he halted beside Janet's wagon and swung to the ground.

He pulled the canvas open at the rear of the wagon. "You lied to me, Janet, honey," he barked. "Now you tell me why they're after Gwen and Ginny." He stared into the wagon, waited for heads to pop up, but he received only silence back. He swung one long leg over the tailgate and climbed into the wagon. "Answer me, dammit," he said as he yanked at a blanket against one side of the wagon.

He stared at the rolled-up sheets underneath it and felt the curse rise in his throat. The damn wagon was empty. Janet had fled with the girls. "Goddamn," he swore. How damn dumb could she be? Or how scared? Fleeing on foot in these wild mountains, he grunted.

Suicide. Yet she plainly knew that being caught meant certain death.

He swung from the wagon, bitterness surging inside him. There was no way to pick up their tracks in the blackness of the night. And they'd had at least an hour's start. Tracking them would have to wait for daylight. But even then, it'd have to wait its turn. Morning would bring more than enough to keep him busy. He sank down against a flat slab of rock, put his head back, and closed his eyes. Morning would come all too quickly.

6

He woke the others at the first gray light of dawn and they faced him with sleep still clinging to them. His words snapped them into instant attention, and when he finished, it was Hurd Bell who broke the silence. "Why don't we just go tell this crew the truth, that Janet and the girls have run off?" he said.

"They won't believe it," Fargo said.

"Then let them come and look for themselves," Bell said.

"No," Howard Galvin cut in quickly. "They'll tear every wagon apart to make sure we're not hiding them. I can't have that."

"There's another reason not to do that," Fargo said. "They didn't just talk about killing the girls. They talked about killing anyone else around."

"So we wind up fighting a bunch of killers over two girls who aren't even here," Galvin said, the irony of it lacing his words.

"Right now you'll be fighting to save your own hides," Fargo said.

"We wait for them to charge us and cut them down?" one of the men asked.

"They won't charge us the way the Shoshoni did. They'll come at us from more than one direction," Fargo said.

"Then all we can do is take cover and fight," Bell said.

"Not from down here. They'll be expecting that, and they'll pick us off even behind the wagons. First, leave the wagons exactly where they are. Roll your blankets up under them and put your hats at the head of each blanket. They'll be in a hurry to shoot and they won't be looking too hard." He paused as his eyes went to the tall rock formations that all but surrounded the campsite. "You start climbing those rocks now. They're full of ridges and craggy places. Find yourselves a spot where you can hang on and fire from. When they come in, we blast them from above. We ought to get most of them."

He turned, strode to the nearest tall rock formation, and watched the others begin to scurry up the other rocks, Lottie pulling herself along in front of Galvin. Fargo began to climb and found a spot not too high up where he could brace one foot against a small protuberance of stone and wedge the other into a fissure. The others were disappearing in the craggy formations, he saw, and he settled down to wait, the Colt in his hand.

The wait was a short one as he spotted the figures on horseback moving through the trees to approach the top of the hillside from both sides. He waited, watching their shadowy shapes come closer as the morning sun rose above the high peaks. They were near the wagons when he spotted the elkskin vest of the horseman to his right. Two others moved up alongside the man and suddenly, at a signal, they charged from the right side, firing at the shapes they saw beneath the wagons. Those on the left side took a few seconds longer to charge, but they too came racing in.

Fargo drew a bead on one figure and fired and the man flew from his horse. At his shot, the tall rock formations erupted in a salvo of gunfire and Fargo saw the men below pull to a halt, wheel in confusion as they were cut down by the withering volleys from above. He saw the mustached man in the elkskin vest clutch at his side, fall half over his horse's neck, and race from the circle. Not more than two or three others were able to flee, and Fargo holstered the Colt as he let himself skid down the side of the rocks.

He jumped the last six feet to the ground, raced for the Ovaro, and leapt into the saddle to send the horse racing down the mountainside. The man in the elkskin vest had been wounded. He wouldn't be riding fast for long, and the few others that remained had probably scattered. A rout usually turned into each man for himself.

Fargo wasn't more than halfway down the mountainside when he caught sight of the elkskin vest, its owner bent over in the saddle and moving slowly. The Trailsman put the pinto into a downhill gallop and caught up to the fleeing figure in seconds. He saw the man turn, pain and fear in his face, and Fargo drew the Colt and fired a shot that purposely grazed his quarry's hat.

"Rein up," he shouted. "I'm only going to say it once." The man looked back, pain pulling at his lips, and he reined to a halt. "Drop your gun," Fargo said, and saw the man toss a side-hammer Jocelyn army revolver to the ground. Fargo came up alongside him, halted, and swung to the ground as the man slid from his horse, one hand clutching his side.

"Jesus, I'm bleeding bad," the man said as he dropped to one knee.

"Take your hand away," Fargo said, and he peered at the wound as the man obeyed. "Nothing torn up. The bullet went in and out. Maybe cracked a rib," he said. "You'll live."

"I've got to find a doc," the man said.

"Not in these mountains. Bandage it tight and you can make it," Fargo said.

"I haven't any damn bandages."

"I've an extra roll in my saddlebag. You start answering some questions and they're yours," Fargo said.

The man glowered at him. "And if I don't?"

"You can drop dead from loss of blood for all I care," Fargo said. He stepped to where the man had tossed the Jocelyn, picked up the gun, emptied it, and flung it a good fifty yards into the thick brush. "Why were you after the girls?" he asked. The man sank down onto the ground as he kept one hand pressed to his side.

"The bandages first. I'm bleeding," he said.

"Answers first," Fargo said. "Why?"

"We were hired," the man said. "By Iris Bailey."

"Who the hell is Iris Bailey?" Fargo frowned.

"Tom Bailey's wife," the man said.

"Make sense," Fargo snapped.

"Tom Bailey was a very big, very respected man back in Colorado, Mayor of Gannon City, the town banker, candidate for governor, church deacon. Then he happened to run into those two little bitches who lived just outside town. Janet Johnson was hired by their father to watch over them—one of those governesses they're called. Their father spent most of his time back East on business. Well, it seems she didn't watch close enough. They wound up having an affair with Tom Bailey, both of them. As I hear tell, they were having a high old time, everything a new experience for them."

"It takes two to tango. Bailey let himself get involved," Fargo said.

"Yes, but when he tried to break it off, they talked, really shot their mouths off, named dates, times, and places. Tom Bailey couldn't take it. He killed himself with a Remington forty-four."

"And the wife blames Gwen and Ginny," Fargo said.

"For everything. For getting her husband into an affair, then by talking about it until he killed himself," the man said.

"So she hired you to kill the girls," Fargo said.

"You've got it," the man said. "But their pa heard about everything and he blamed Janet Johnson for everything. He said if she'd done her job, the girls wouldn't have gotten to Tom Bailey. He told her to get the girls to the mission school in Washington or he'd have her ass."

"Iris Bailey tell you to kill Janet, too?" Fargo asked.

"Iris Bailey's a woman with a howling revenge inside her. We got orders to kill anybody connected with those bitches. But when the Johnson woman ran with them, it took us a spell to track down where she was headed."

Fargo walked to the pinto, rummaged in his saddlebag, and found the roll of bandages. He tossed them at the man's feet. "You're lucky, mister. People that come trying to kill me usually end up that way," he said, contempt in his voice as he swung onto the pinto and rode away. His thoughts tumbled as he rode up the mountainside.

Janet had tossed him a few selected kernels of fact while she'd lied about the real truth. And now she had run with the girls, driven by fear and self-preservation. To run was the only thing left for her, she had concluded. Stay alive, hide and then go on somehow. The logic of desperation. But on her own in these mountains, without a horse or a wagon, was only postponing death for herself and the girls. When he reached the circle of rocks, his jaw was set and he rode to a halt as the others rushed forward.

"We did it," Howard Galvin shouted gleefully. "Nobody's been scratched here. Now we can go on."

"I'm going after Janet and the girls," he said.

"What?" Galvin frowned.

"They're as good as dead if I can't find them," Fargo said.

"They made their own bed, whatever it was. They can lie in it," Galvin said. "I want these wagons in Colfax. Every damn minute counts."

"I'll get you there," Fargo said.

"I didn't pay to have you do good deeds, dammit," Galvin thundered.

"I saved your neck a few times. I'm all paid up in that department," Fargo said.

"Indeed you are," Lottie cut in. "Go try to find them."

"I'll be back," Fargo said as he wheeled the horse and moved to Janet's wagon. He leaned from the saddle as he searched the ground. He spotted the footprints, finally, three sets moving into the trees, and he saw that they had set off across the center of a steep mountainside. The Ovaro moved gingerly and Fargo let him pick and choose his own way. He knew no other horse that could handle moving sideways across the steepness. Janet had led the way, he saw, a smart move. It was unlikely her pursuers would find the tracks, and even more unlikely they'd be able to cross their horses after them. The slope came to an end and leveled off into a forest heavy with red cedar and ponderosa.

The footprints became single-file and he slowed at a spot where they halted and the forest floor was flattened down in three places. They'd stopped to sleep there and he spied the footprints where they continued on through the forest. He'd followed for perhaps another three hours, making good time tracking the clear prints. He was closing on them, the footprints growing fresh, when he caught the odor of smoke and reined to a halt. He let his nostrils draw in another deep draft of air. No camp fire. Chimney smoke, unmistakable in its combination of burning wood, caked ash, tar, and hot stone. He followed his nose and moved to the right through the trees and his brow wrinkled as suddenly there were not three sets of footprints but six, the new ones fashioned of heavy-soled boots.

As apprehension curled around him, he slowed, the trees thinning, and he saw the cleared section of land with three ramshackle huts in a semicircle, patched roofs, and doors hanging from their hinges. A wisp of smoke curled from the short, stone chimney of one hut, and his lips drew back in a grimace as his gaze took in the scene in front of the huts. Gwen, Ginny, and Janet were in the center of a semicircle of figures, six men in just long johns or tattered shirts and stained trousers. All wore straggly beards and long, uncombed hair. He saw four women in torn garments, four half-naked youngsters running around one another. He saw a half-dozen chickens and three mud-encrusted hogs. A movement alongside one of the huts caught his eye and he glimpsed two young boys looking on, sixteen years old, he guessed.

Fargo returned his eyes to the circle of figures. Mountain people, in all their feral unsavoriness. As he scanned the figures again, he recognized the one he had run into near the lake.

A tall man wearing only trousers examined Ginny and Gwen with a leering smile of anticipation on a gaunt, straggly-bearded face. "My, I do believe this is our lucky day," he said. "We got us something special."

"We gonna keep them, aren't we, Abel?" one of the others said.

"Of course we're gonna keep them. Why wouldn't we?" the one called Abel answered.

"You'll do nothing of the sort. You'll let us go this very minute," Fargo heard Janet cut in. Maybe she was quaking with fear, but she didn't let it show and he gave her credit for that, Fargo noted.

But Abel threw a hard glance at her. "We're gonna have to teach you to mind your mouth," he said. The four women's worn, haggard, and unkempt appearance made them seem almost the same age as they joined together in a sharp cackle. Out of the corner of his eye, Fargo saw the two youths move forward from the side of the hut and suddenly another man appeared, heavier than the others, with a torn undershirt covering a sizable paunch. A rifle in the crook of one arm, he carried two slain black-tailed jackrabbits by their ears.

Fargo had his hand resting on the Colt at his side but he drew it away. He could easily bring down a few with his first salvo, but the girls and Janet were too much in the center of the half-circle and two of the men held long-barreled, rifled muskets. They were all crack shots, these mountain men, and they'd not hesitate to shoot their captives.

He had to get a better hand, his own cards to hold, Fargo knew. Even the wildest of creatures cares for its own. He moved the horse forward. He had to get closer, he realized. He watched Abel draw his hand along Ginny's face, down to her neck, and then across her breasts.

"Get away from me," Ginny said with cold ice in her voice, but Abel only laughed, a deep, guttural sound.

As Fargo moved out of the trees he saw everyone turn, the mountain folk with surprise and frowns, Janet and the girls with relief. He walked the horse into the semicircle and dismounted as he saw the mountain people stare with hostility in their eyes.

"Damn, it's shit full of strangers around here all of a sudden," Abel rasped.

"It's him, goddamn, Abel. It's him," Fargo heard the voice cut in, and he saw the man from the lake step forward. "He's the one I told you about." Abel's eyes hardened on Fargo as the other man danced forward again. "He took my knife. Be careful, Abel, he's real tricky."

Abel's eyes peered at the big man with the lake-blue eyes. "What are you doin' here, stranger?" he asked.

Fargo gestured to Janet and the girls. "They got themselves lost. I've been trailing them to bring them back."

"Well, now they got themselves found," Abel said with a leering smile.

"I'll be taking them along," Fargo said quietly.

"Hell you will," Abel said, his voice hardening. Fargo saw the three men with the rifles start to swing their guns around. Abel cupped his hand under Gwen's breast again. "We're gonna have us a high old time riding these two. They're ripe and ready," he gloated.

"She's only eighteen. She's just a child," Janet said. "Have you no sense of decency?"

"Old enough to bleed, old enough to breed," Abel said.

Fargo shot a glance at Janet. "One of those other viewpoints," he commented blandly, and she managed a glare. He let his eyes sweep the children again and his gaze followed one, a girl some eight or nine years old, he guessed. It was hard to see past the dirt on her face and the one-piece cotton dress and unwashed blond hair. He returned his eyes to Abel.

"How about I just take them and leave?" he asked.

"How about you get your ass out of here before we shoot it off," Abel barked, and Fargo saw two of the others raise their long-barrel muskets. He shrugged and saw the disbelief in Janet's face as he obediently pulled himself onto the pinto.

"Guess I wasted my time," he said from the saddle.

"You just forget about these three peaches, mister, you hear me?" Abel warned as Fargo slowly turned the pinto.

The dirty-faced blond girl was but a few feet from him, tugging at a piece of stock with a smaller child. Fargo moved the horse sideways, a few steps closer to her, and cast a glance at Abel and the others. They were watching him, but they had relaxed some, as it appeared that he was leaving. He moved the horse another step sideways, half-turned toward Abel; then, with a lightninglike swoop of one long arm, he swept the girl up into the saddle in front of him. His other hand had drawn the Colt at the same instant and now the muzzle of the revolver pressed into the child's temple.

But one of the men had reacted fast to seize Janet, yank her against him as he put the musket to her throat. Fargo flicked a glance at the man and Janet's panic-stricken face and brought his gaze back to Abel. "I leave with them or the little girl's dead," he said.

"You shoot her and Zeb's gonna blow that little lady's skull off," Abel countered. Fargo swore inwardly and fought away the dryness in his throat. He had to play his hand out. There was no other choice. If he backed down, they'd shoot him anyway. "Looks as like we've a Chinese standoff here, mister," Abel said.

"Not to me," Fargo said, and saw the man's eyes narrow in thought. "She's a job. She's no kin," he said. "You call it."

Abel's eyes held on him and suddenly one of the women cried out. "Pa, you can't let him kill Enid. She's our firstborn," the woman said.

Fargo kept his face impassive, almost uncaring, but Abel's lips twitched as fury and family fought inside him. "Hurry up. My job, your kid. Call it," Fargo said, and let the sound of the gun hammer being drawn back add emphasis to his words.

Abel made a growling sound in his throat. "Let the damn bitch go," he called to the man holding Janet. The man flung her from him with such force that she went down hard with a yelp of pain. She pushed to her feet and Fargo saw she was limping.

"Help her," he barked at Gwen and Ginny, and they rushed to take hold of her on both sides. "Walk. Back the way you came," Fargo said. Janet between them, they walked into the trees. Fargo kept the Colt against the child's temple.

"Let her go. You got yours," Abel demanded.

"And have you blast me apart?" Fargo answered. "Not yet. I'll let her go when I'm out of here." He saw the fury in Abel's eyes as Fargo backed the Ovaro toward the trees, moved into the curtain of foliage, and wheeled the horse in a tight circle. He rode perhaps a thousand yards through the trees when he halted and let the little girl slide to the ground. She raced away at once and Fargo turned and quickly caught up to Gwen, Ginny, and Janet.

"God, were we glad to see you," Ginny breathed, and he saw the pain in Janet's face as she limped along.

"Get in the saddle," he said as he swung to the

ground. She carefully pulled herself onto the horse. He set off in a trot and Gwen and Ginny stayed but a few paces behind him as the Ovaro casually loped alongside. His eyes searched the forest and he suddenly called a halt as he glimpsed three moss-covered fallen trees that had probably once been struck by lightning. He moved the Ovaro around to the other side of the trees and offered Janet a hand in dismounting. She accepted and winced in pain as she touched down. "Hunker down behind the logs, all of you," he said.

"They're coming after us?" Janet asked, fear instant in her voice.

"They'll give it a try," he said. "Abel can't just let us go. He'd lose face." He led the pinto deeper into the trees until the horse was out of sight and then returned to the logs where the others were lying flat. The big Sharps in one hand, he lowered himself to the ground beside Janet.

"What happened back at camp?" she asked.

"You mean did that posse chasing you wipe out everybody?" Fargo shot back, and she made no reply for a long moment.

"I hope that didn't happen," she murmured.

"You didn't do anything to help stop it, did you, such as telling me the truth," he said harshly.

"When you left, I was afraid. The only thing I could think of was to run," she said. "I didn't know what else to do."

"Truth never seems to cross your mind, does it, honey?" he said.

She fell silent again. "You know now they were after us," she said.

"Bull's-eye," he growled, and spotted the first shadowy shape moving through the trees. "Shut up and keep down," he said. He brought the big Sharps up to rest atop the log.

Two figures, then a third, and a distance behind, a fourth. They were moving too quickly, too certain their quarry was still fleeing. They weren't real hunters. Small game and an occasional deer was their meat. They were mountain people, inbred, amoral, only able to survive in their own ways. It wouldn't even take a lot to send them packing.

Fargo brought his eye down to the sight on the rifle as the first two figures came closer. One was the man from the lake, the other the one that had seized hold of Janet. He let them come a little closer, drew a bead on the man from the lake, and fired.

"Oh, Jesus, my leg," the man screamed as he went down.

Fargo saw the other figure half-rise, peer into the trees, and the big Sharps barked again. The man went down clutching his shoulder with an oath of pain. Fargo saw the other two halt, drop low, and then heard both of the men he'd wounded pulling their way along the ground.

"Give us a hand. Shit, over here," one cried out, and Fargo glimpsed the other two figures, crouched low, hurrying to help the first two.

He lowered the rifle and watched the rescuers half-drag the two wounded men into the thick trees. He listened to the sounds of their retreat and heard another voice join their muttered oaths.

"They won't be back," he said. "They're not the kind to follow up." He let another moment go and then rose and pulled Janet up with him. She winced and he helped her to the horse.

"My ankle. It's swollen," she said. "It hurts real bad."

"You can put compresses on it when we get back," he said, and returned the rifle to its saddle holster. Gwen and Ginny came alongside him as he held the pace to a walk this time. He cast a glance at Janet as she rode, the ankle plainly bothering her. "Nobody's going to be happy with you," he said.

She returned a tight-lipped glance. "I'm sorry about that, but I'll live with it. I'm here to get Gwen and

Ginny to the mission school. Everything else comes after," she said.

"I know everything," Fargo said. "I convinced one of the posse to loosen his tongue. You should've told me the truth before we started."

"I was afraid you wouldn't take me, then," Janet said. "It's all past now. I just want to go on."

"You can drop all that she's-just-a-child shit," Fargo said.

"It's true. They both are," Janet said.

"Only by the calendar," Fargo grunted, and heard giggles from Ginny and Gwen.

Janet fell silent and he halted twice to let her rest. There were still a few hours of day left when they reached the site and the waiting wagons. Janet received mostly grim stares as she limped into the wagon, except for Lottie.

"Glad you made it back," she said, and Janet looked gratefully back at her.

Fargo saw Gwen and Ginny climb onto the driver's seat and Gwen took the reins, both flashing him wide smiles. He decided they couldn't smile any other way but provocatively, and he stepped to the rear of the wagon to see that Janet was seated with a compress of cold water on her ankle. She glanced up at him and there was sincerity mixed in with the exhaustion and pain in her face.

"You didn't have to come after us," she murmured. "Thank you. You're a man of surprises."

"I'm not in your league, honey," he said. "If you've any more, I want to hear about them now."

"No, nothing more. You said you knew everything. That's all there is," Janet said.

He nodded and returned to the pinto. "Roll," he called, and set out down the slope. He found a slanting cut that ran between two towering crags, and when dusk descended, he had picked out a spot where the land widened into a stretch of forest, mostly Douglas fir and hackberry. He had the wagons pull into a wide circle, and after a sparse meal Galvin paused as he walked to his wagon.

"I don't want any more delays. She could still be lying to you," the man said.

"Can't say for sure, but I don't think so," Fargo replied. "The truth is, with all that's happened, we're still making good time."

"How come?" Galvin frowned as Lottie came along.

"Because Fargo's been finding passages through these damn mountains," Lottie put in.

"I never argue with a lady." Fargo grinned and Galvin strode away muttering under his breath.

Lottie turned her eyes on Fargo. "I was right," she said, and he lifted an eyebrow. "About their not being after Howie. I just knew."

"I didn't buy that then. I don't now," Fargo said pleasantly.

She shrugged, nodded back, and walked away.

Fargo took his bedroll and went deep into the trees and stretched his things out. He undressed; the night was staying warm and his thoughts wandered. First the Boxleys, now Janet. Was there one more surprise waiting that carried Galvin's name? He'd almost wager on it, but he didn't want to draw trouble to himself. Superstitious, he grunted, ashamed of himself. Yet the feelings stayed, and he was still turning them in his mind when he heard the footsteps moving through the trees.

He lifted himself onto one elbow, not surprised by the visit and the figure took shape and came toward him. Clad in white shirt and black skirt, Ginny came to a halt, and the provocative smile toyed with her lips as her eyes swept across his body.

"You draw straws again?" Fargo asked, and she nodded.

"I won this time," she said. "I came to thank you for coming after us today." She dropped to her knees beside him, her eyes moving across his muscled frame. "And I thought I'd stay awhile," she said.

"Last time, when Gwen came up, Janet came looking for her," Fargo said.

"Janet's fast asleep tonight," Ginny said, and with quick movements her fingers unbuttoned the white shirt and she whisked it away. The skirt followed and she had nothing beneath either.

He found himself marveling at the utter beauty of her nubile body, like Gwen's, full-breasted with faint-pink nipples and beautifully curved white mounds, and a slightly convex little belly with a curly, dense triangle beneath it. But again, as with her sister's body, she glowed with a throbbing sensuousness. Nakedness seemed to trigger her eagerness, for he saw her lips part and heard her breath come in short, gasping sounds. She almost fell atop him as she came forward, her mouth open as it closed onto his and her tongue darting at once with frantic eagerness.

Her breasts came against his chest, warm, soft, the pink nipples tiny little pressure points into his skin. "God, yes, yes," Ginny breathed, and her hands began to move up and down his body. Her lips implored, wet with wanting. He finally brought his mouth down to one beautiful, full-cupped breast and Ginny gave a half-scream at the touch. He let his tongue caress the faint pink tip, slide back and forth across it, and felt it rise in response. Ginny's hips were moving, a slow, writhing motion, and her hands had come to clasp his buttocks.

"Take me, God, take me," she whispered, and he brought his own hot wanting over her pubic mound. She cried out again as her hands dug into his sides. She writhed under him, legs and hips moving together, her black, curly nap lifting, falling back, moving under him again. Serpentlike, her full-fleshed body turned, twisted, came up against him. Low, guttural sounds were coming from her in a steady stream. He moved, brought himself down in between her legs, and felt the wetness of her at once. "Jesus, please, please, oh, yes, yes," Ginny half-whispered, her voice tight.

He let himself go forward, slide into the liquid-coated tunnel, and Ginny screamed, a cry that rose up from the guttural sounds, made of pure delight. She moved with him, hips twisting, rotating in a half-circle. He thrust again and then again. She answered each thrust with her own surging motion as she pulled his head down to her breasts. "Ah, ah, aaaaah," Ginny breathed, the low moaning sounds returning, and he felt the glowing heat of her against him, flesh melting into flesh, her thighs moving against his hips, rubbing back and forth, her entire ripe young body aflame with surging heat.

He felt himself brought spiraling by her sinuous eroticism and he only barely managed to hold back until he suddenly felt her surging increase, grow stronger and quicker. "Oh, oh, aaaaagh, ah, now, now . . . Jesus, now," Ginny screamed, her voice rising in a crescendo of ecstasy, and he felt himself explode with her and she clung and twisted and still surged as the climax of shudders ran through her.

Finally, with a tremendous groaning sound, she went limp and fell back onto the bedroll, her thighs loosening from around him but her full-cupped breasts still quivering. He stayed with her a moment longer and met her eyes as a tiny smile edged her lips. Something more than satisfaction, a quiet triumph in it, he decided.

She uttered a deep sigh and pushed to a sitting position as she reached out to take her shirt. She slipped it on, the gorgeous breasts vanishing behind the material, followed with the skirt. She rose to her feet with a quick swing of her hips and seemed schoolgirllike as she swung around to face him. "It was great," she said.

"It was," he agreed.

"Don't go to sleep right away," Ginny said.

"Wasn't planning to," Fargo returned, and she blew him a kiss as she hurried into the trees.

He lay back, letting the warm night air caress his body. He was smiling when he heard the footsteps approach through the trees. It had taken only a little longer than he'd expected. He sat up as Gwen hurried to him. She wore a blue robe with nothing underneath it. It dropped to the ground and he knew he was staring, but not just at the luscious loveliness of her. She was a physical echo, a fleshy duplication of Ginny, the same full deep breasts, the same light-pink, small nipples, same full smooth thighs, little convex belly, and only her curly, dark nap was somewhat smaller. And like Ginny, she fairly glowed with throbbing sensuousness, sending out waves of it even standing still.

But she didn't stand still long. She dropped to her knees and her hands reached out, seized him as he responded to the force of her. "Jesus, oh, yes, oh, oh, oooooh," Gwen breathed, and pulled him to her. Her hands caressed his pulsating maleness as she pushed her breasts into his face and he took first one, then the other, and she cried out in small gasps. He rolled with her as she came atop him, brought her pelvis down over him, found his seeking spear, and sank onto him with a scream of sheer delight. But the physical echo ended in the act of making love. Where Ginny had been all sinuousity, Gwen was all frantic bouncy pushing, wild thrustings in place of smooth surging, high-pitched gasped cries instead of low moans.

Erotic energies in a different form, he realized through his pleasure, yet the same in content, suffusing their entire bodies, erupting from their innermost wantings. There was one more difference. Gwen climaxed much more quickly, pulling him with her onto his side, then pumping furiously as he straddled her. He felt himself swept up in her wildness, her short, staccato screams, and then suddenly he was with her as she shook and quivered and screamed into his chest as she clung to him. "Oh, God," Gwen breathed as the moment of moments exploded and finally spiraled away. She held on to him as she drew in deep drafts of air. The same but different, Fargo mused silently as he enjoyed the beauty of her. Finally Gwen disentangled herself from him. The same smile of quiet triumph touched her lips as she pulled the robe around herself.

"We've got to find another night," Gwen said.

"That might not be so easy," he said.

"We'll see," she said, and walked from him with slow steps, wrapped in her own world.

Fargo lay back and drew a deep breath of his own as he tried to find words for Gwen and Ginny. They were more than precocious. And more than just a pair of sex-kittens. There was no predatoriness about them, no coy masking of their throbbing wants. They had a certain purity of erotic energy, he decided, two volcanoes too hot not to boil over. It was no wonder their father had hired a governess for them, and even less wonder that Janet had failed.

Janet still refused to recognize Gwen and Ginny for what they were. Probably because she refused to let herself recognize the existence of such unvarnished erotic emotion. Without recognition, she'd never understand. Or perhaps she simply refused to admit its existence. Admitting could bring other problems. What you admitted in others, you had to examine in yourself. The mission school would be good for Gwen and Ginny, difficult but good, and not only for their safety. They needed harnessing, a time to let maturity add reins to their urges.

But they had surely made a memorable night. He smiled as he went to sleep.

7

Morning came in with a hot sun, and when Fargo returned to the wagons, he found everyone ready to roll.

Janet wore a bandage strapped around her ankle, he noted, but the solid night's sleep had erased the drawn lines in her face. He saw her frown as Gwen and Ginny waved happily at him.

Howard Galvin drove his wagon, Lottie beside him, and Janet swung in behind as Fargo led the way along the stretch of land. He rode ahead, his eyes searching the terrain. They were in the heart of the towering mountain range now, the great peaks looming on all sides. The mountains always made him realize how puny man was, and indeed how clumsy a creature he was as a herd of bighorn sheep leapt from crag to crag with effortless grace.

The towering peaks were insurmountable even for horse and rider, to say nothing of wagons, but he spotted another cut through the distant crags. The closer land rose with a cluster of firs and he waited until the others caught up to him and pointed to the distant cut. Once again he rode ahead, then glanced back to see that the heavy drays were able to climb the sharp rise. He reached the top of the rise and saw a long, wide stretch of flatland open up ahead, directly in line with the distant cut through the peaks. He reined up and let his gaze sweep the terrain on both sides of the wide stretch of land. Both were heavily forested with Douglas fir, hackberry, and ponderosa. To go around the flat expanse of tangled brush and move through the trees would take the better part of the day. To go straight across the brush-covered level land would bring them to the distant cut hours earlier.

Yet he stayed motionless, staring across the land that was mostly thick, low mountain brush, easy enough for the wagons to handle. An inner sense told him to take the longer, harder way, and he frowned as he stared ahead. The brush-covered passage seemed too easy, too much a gift. An inconsequential reason, he admitted, making little sense. But then he had supplied the reason when reason played no part in his feelings. He still stared across the brush-covered, wide stretch as the others caught up to him and rolled to a halt.

"We'll go around it and through the forest," Fargo said.

"What?" Galvin barked. "Why in hell for?"

"I don't know," Fargo said honestly. "But I don't like it."

"Hell, we'll lose a whole day that way," Galvin protested. "I'm not going to do that."

"We go around," Fargo said. "I've a feeling about it."

"Goddamn, I'm not interested in your feelings. Can you give me one concrete reason not to go ahead?" Galvin barked.

"No," Fargo admitted.

"Then I'm going straight on, dammit. I told you, time's important," Galvin barked.

Fargo glanced at Lottie and saw the uncertainty in her eyes. Finally she shrugged and he turned away.

"Let's roll," the Trailsman said as he grimaced and swallowed the unformed misgivings inside himself. He rode over to one side where he had a better overall view of the stretch of land while Galvin and the others move directly through the center. He stayed perhaps a hundred yards ahead and to the side as he walked the pinto on across the land and took in the thick mountain brush. A variety of low plant and bush species mingled in with the brush, and he noted knotweed, mountain laurel, possumhaw, and the shiny red berries of bittersweet nightshade. The stretch of terrain was lush with growth, and as he rode on, he began to wonder if his inner sense hadn't betrayed him this time. He glanced at the wagons, still some hundred yards to his left but almost parallel with him now as he let the pinto amble slowly forward.

He brought his eyes back to the land that stretched out in front of him, the cut in the mountain still only a distant ribbon. He found himself sweeping a sudden wide growth of sedges and felt a tiny furrow touch his brow. He pushed on and found himself staring at a thick expanse of skunk cabbage, the mottled purplish-green leaves easy to spot along with their brown-and-yellow pearlike buds. The furrow on his brow deepened, and when he saw the delicate, wispy white flower clusters of the highly poisonous water hemlock, the furrow became a beetling frown.

"Sedges, skunk cabbage, water hemlock," he muttered aloud as the realization exploded inside him. Those were plants that grew only in one kind of soil: wetlands, swamplands, marshes, and bogs. "Shit," he exploded, and wheeled the Ovaro around. His inner sense hadn't failed him at all, he grunted in satisfaction, and he was in a gallop when he reached the wagons and waved them to a halt. "Turn around. You're in a mountain bog," he shouted. "Another fifty yards and you'll be sinking out of sight."

Galvin pulled to a stop and frowned at him, then peered ahead. "I don't see any damn bog," he said.

"I don't, either," Fargo said.

"Then how can you be so damn sure?" the man persisted.

"You see smoke, you know there's fire," Fargo

said. "Of course, you have to be able to recognize smoke."

"What's that mean?" Galvin frowned.

"It means he recognized marsh plants," Lottie put in, her eyes on Fargo.

"Bull's-eye," Fargo said.

"That's why he's the Trailsman," Lottie said. "Turn the wagon around, Howard, and be damn grateful."

Galvin muttered sounds under his breath, but he began to turn his wagon and the others followed.

"We go back and take the long way around," Fargo said.

"We'll have lost another four hours now," Galvin grumbled.

"It was your choice, mister," Fargo said, and Lottie tossed him a quick smile. He winked at her, and the converted grocery wagon moved back the way it had come while the others slowly turned and followed. Janet slowed as she passed him.

"You are good, aren't you?" she said, no edge to her tone.

"At all kinds of things," he answered.

There was a torrent of giggles from Gwen and Ginny. Janet frowned at them and threw a glance at Fargo that still held the frown before she drove on.

It was past midday when they reached the line of trees that circled the bog and Fargo called a halt to rest the horses. He slumped down against a tree trunk and saw Janet watching him with a tiny furrow across her forehead as Gwen and Ginny lay down on a bed of panic grass a few dozen yards away. "You want to tell me?" he asked mildly.

"Tell you what?" Janet returned.

"What bee you have in your bonnet," he said.

She nodded to where Ginny and Gwen lay on the grass. "They're chipper as larks today," she muttered.

"That mean something?" Fargo asked mildly.

"It might. It has in the past, though I didn't realize

it then," Janet said. "I was so exhausted last night I didn't check on them as I usually do." She paused and focused a frown on Fargo. "I keep remembering that visit Gwen paid you. I'm still not sure you don't agree with the attitude of those hillbillies."

"You've a suspicious turn of mind, Janet," Fargo commented.

"Perhaps they've made me that way. Perhaps everything has," she said. "I just hope they obeyed my orders last night."

"What'd you tell them?" he queried.

"Forget about all the bad things that have happened and imagine good things, pleasant things," she said.

"That's good advice. I think you can rest assured they took you up on it," Fargo said, and pushed to his feet. "Time to roll," he said, and strode to the Ovaro. He smiled inwardly as he climbed into the saddle. He had seen it again. Janet knew her little charges were sexual time bombs, but she still refused to recognize the fact. She continued to want to see them as little girls merely needing guidance. She refused to recognize the existence of pure erotic energy. She was afraid, and not really for Gwen and Ginny.

He led the way until dark began to fall, and unable to find any good place to camp, he simply called a halt amid the giant ponderosa pines. He took his bedroll only a dozen feet from the others this time and slept at once, certain there'd be no unexpected visitors this night.

When morning came, he rode on ahead, the cut taking real shape now. It was wide enough but steep and he saw a half-dozen narrower passages that branched off from both sides. He chose one that was less steep; he climbed higher and found a ledge that looked down on the terrain below and behind. He swept the land only once with his piercing gaze when he spotted the distant movement. Another posse of riders. He frowned. More than the others. Perhaps twice as many.

They were still moving down one of the distant slopes and it seemed they were following the wagon tracks. He couldn't be certain of that yet, but he'd have more than a few hours to decide. He returned to where the others had reached the cut, and led them up the steepness until he reached the branch that was narrower but easier for the horses to climb. The passage ran for a dozen miles, wandered its way through rock sides and pine-covered earthen walls.

He rode ahead again, explored first one direction and then another until he found another passage. It was into the afternoon when he scaled a high place again and peered back at the following riders. They had gained ground, but they were still not at the mountain bog and they'd not be close enough before night fell. But he could get a better estimate of their number and he guessed at least fifteen, perhaps twenty.

There was also no question now that they were following the wagon tracks, but he waited until the day drew to an end and the wagons camped in a square of land rimmed by tall rocks before he faced the others.

"There's another posse chasing after us," he announced.

Janet's eyes widened in surprise. Howard Galvin frowned and glared at her. Lottie kept her face expressionless.

"What have you done this time, girl?" Galvin barked at Janet.

"Nothing. They're not after me . . . us," she said. "There wouldn't be two of them."

"There might be. I hear Iris Bailey is a woman bound for revenge," Fargo said, his words really tossed out to draw further reaction.

"Of course, that has to be it," Howard Galvin said at once.

Fargo smiled inwardly. He had gotten his answer.

The man had been too quick to seize on his speculation, too eager to indict Janet again.

"Then again, maybe not," Fargo said casually. "This bunch is more than twice as big as the last one. I'd guess they're after bigger fish to fry." He glanced at Lottie, who looked away.

"Meaning what exactly, Fargo?" Galvin bristled.

"Maybe wagons with secret cargo," Fargo said.

"They're not after me," Galvin insisted. "But if they are by some mistake, we still have to fight them off. The last ones were going to kill everybody, not just Janet and the girls. What makes you think these will be different?"

Fargo smiled. The man's argument was completely self-serving, yet completely sound. "You're right there. I've no choice but to go with that possibility," he admitted.

"So find a place to make a stand," Galvin said.

"That won't be enough. This'll take something special, a special place and a special way to make a fight," Fargo said.

"Why? We just hole up and fight them off," Galvin said.

Fargo's glance was chiding. "You're down to four men. You and I make it six with four women. And you're going to shoot it out with an armed posse of twenty?" he said, and saw Galvin look uncomfortable. "Get some sleep. I want to be moving by dawn," he finished, and turned away. Lottie passed near and he paused. "You were so sure the last ones weren't after Howie. Nothing to say this time?" he asked.

"I had a feeling last time. I don't always get them," Lottie said.

His smile took the edge from his words and he kept his voice soft. "Bullshit, honey. You knew the last ones weren't after Howie because there weren't enough of them," he said.

"No," she murmured, and shook her tight, blond

curls. She started to hurry away when he caught her arm. She had always been on the verge of confiding in him, always uneasy in her concern for Galvin.

"Talk to me, Lottie. What's going on?" he asked. "You wanted special help from me. I have to know what it's all about."

"Now who's offering deals?" she said, bitterness edging her voice. She pulled her arm from his grip and strode to the wagon. She was afraid, but there was loyalty, perhaps love, inside her. It was stronger than the fear.

Fargo took his bedroll and again stayed near the wagons, quickly drew sleep to himself, and was dressed when the first gray streaks of dawn painted the sky. The sun had yet to clear the tall peaks when he had the wagons moving through the passage. He put the pinto into a canter and found a spot that let him survey the land behind. He found the pursuing riders at once. They had just reached the edge of the mountain bog. They'd see the wagon tracks turn around and circle the bog. He had another four or five hours, he knew, and he moved down to see the wagons and waved them on.

It was perhaps another ten miles on that he found another pass through the mountains and led the wagons into it as his eyes scanned the cliffs and crags. The day moved into the afternoon. Their pursuers would be drawing close, he knew, and he swore as he'd found no place to make a stand. He went on for another hour when he spotted a narrow, sharp incline moving up one side of the mountain. Just wide enough for the big drays to move up single-file, one side was bordered with rock crags, the other dropped off in a steep slope peppered with huge boulders. Fargo took the incline to the top and found a wide, rock table of land that dug into the side of the towering peak but went nowhere. It was, he guessed, probably the result of some ancient movement of the mountains.

But it was exactly what he'd been searching for. He sent the Ovaro back down the narrow incline and waited for the others to arrive. Galvin's wagon in the lead, they finally rolled to a halt and Fargo pointed up the narrow incline.

"Single file to the top," he said.

"What's at the top?" Galvin asked.

"A flat table of rock, enough to take all the wagons," Fargo said.

"We'd be trapped up there." Galvin frowned.

"We could be," Fargo admitted. "But I've other ideas. This is the only place I've found that'll give us an edge."

"Damn, I don't see anything but being trapped," Galvin protested.

"I'll explain when we get up there. I've no time now. They're damn near on our heels," Fargo snapped. "Move."

Lottie snapped the reins over the horses as Howard was about to argue further, the gesture one of confidence and impatience.

Fargo waved Janet on after her and then watched the three big drays move slowly up the incline in single file, the passage just wide enough to accommodate them with enough room for a man on foot alongside. He watched as the big wagons reached the top and disappeared over the crest before he sent the pinto up the incline again.

"Dammit, Fargo, this is a death trap," Galvin burst out as the Ovaro reached the table of rock.

"For them, I hope," Fargo said as he dismounted. "We haven't the firepower to shoot it out. We've got to take most of them out with one blow. We'll use one of your big drays to do it. Pick out the one."

"Use one of my wagons?" Galvin frowned again.

"The only way they can get up here is by the incline. We unhitch the team, roll the wagon to the edge, and send it down. It'll be traveling like a buffalo stampede in seconds. A few may jump over the side, but there's no place to go on that incline. It'll barrel over most of them."

"Damn, it might just work," Hurd Bell said as Galvin frowned in thought.

"What'll happen to the wagon?" Galvin asked.

"It may go over the side, crash into the rock wall on the other side, or roll to the bottom. I don't know and I don't give a damn. It's the wagon or our necks. Pick one or I will," Fargo said.

Galvin nodded to the nearest dray and Bell and the other men quickly unhitched the team. Fargo lent his shoulder to the task of pushing the heavy wagon to the top of the incline. "I'm going down and wait. I'll find a place to hide. At my shot, you send the wagon over," Fargo said.

"Got it," Hurd said, and Fargo's glance at Lottie saw her face filled with anxiety and tension. Her eyes met his and he caught a flicker of something that seemed almost regret. His eyes moved to Janet, her face tight.

"Good luck," she said. Beside her, Ginny and Gwen smiled with a shared privacy.

"We'll be waiting," Ginny said.

Fargo nodded and walked to where the big dray stood poised to roll. He squeezed past the wagon and began to hurry down the incline. Halfway down he halted, spied a boulder a dozen feet down the steep side, and lowered himself to the ground. He slid over the edge on the seat of his pants and used his hands and feet to slow his descent. Reaching the boulder, he slid around to the other side and dug in behind the tall rock from where he could see up to the narrow incline. He relaxed and waited and heard the sound from the incline before he saw the figures. The stab of surprise pushed at him. He counted eighteen figures, all on foot, all carrying carbines. Smart, he grunted. Whoever led them had some brains between his ears.

His men were more maneuverable on foot than they would be charging up the narrow incline on horseback.

But they were no less vulnerable to what he had arranged for them, Fargo knew. He drew the Colt as the men came almost abreast of him, trotting up the incline in twos and threes. He let them go past before he took aim at one of the figures bringing up the rear. He fired and the man's arms flew into the air as the heavy bullet smashed into him. Fargo saw the others duck and turn in surprise, unsure where the shot had been fired from. They were still in their crouched position, still scanning the sides of the incline, when he heard the roaring rumble that instantly grew louder.

The men turned, stared up at the incline ahead of them just as the huge wagon appeared, rolling downhill at full speed.

Fargo watched as they spun, suddenly in panic as they realized there was no room to run. He saw one man flatten himself against the rock side of the incline as the big dray thundered past him, but the others tried to flee ahead of it or get out of its way. Neither choice worked on the narrow incline, and Fargo winced as he listened to the screams of those crushed by the heavy wagon. Some got in each other's way as they attempted to run, and paid the price. He saw three men leap from the incline and roll headlong down the steep side. One smashed into a boulder and lay still, but the other two managed to keep rolling.

The sudden sound of splintering wood brought Fargo's eyes back to the incline and he saw that the wagon had smashed into the stone wall on the other side of the path. The front wheels buckled and it came to rest with one corner against the stone. A few men, three in all, had managed to avoid the thundering wagon and were racing down the incline. Fargo held back firing. There was no need. All they wanted was to get to the bottom of the incline. He rose and watched as one of the men slowed to go to the aid of another in a red-checked shirt who had stumbled to one knee in pain.

"Harry, help me with the sheriff," he heard the man call out as the third figure went to his aid.

Fargo stared at the three men as they helped the third man down the path. "Sheriff," the Trailsman murmured aloud, the word reverberating inside him. His initial surprise had already begun to turn to dismay and then into a mixture of cold fury and self-reproach. "Sheriff," he murmured aloud again. "A goddamn sheriff's posse." He swore silently. He hadn't considered that possibility, not after the hired guns that had come after Janet. But Galvin had to have known. He knew the posse was after him, just as Lottie knew. And he had to have been pretty damn certain who they were, Fargo swore. Damn his weaseling, lying hide!

But Galvin had maintained his front of innocence and silence and now the land was littered with slain men, perhaps men who had done nothing more than what they thought was right at the recruitment of the law. Fargo glanced up at the tall peaks already covered by dusk. Night wasn't more than a half-hour away. The sheriff and those left alive would stay the night and tend to their wounds at the bottom of the incline. They'd be retrieving their dead in the morning, and Fargo swore silently again. He had to find out more, he knew as the cold rage churned inside him. He had to find out what it all meant, the truth of it and whether he'd been taken in by a conspiracy of cleverness and deceit.

But there'd be no finding the truth from Howard Galvin. All he'd get there were more evasions. He'd not give the man the satisfaction of asking. Only the men at the bottom of the incline might furnish truth. But not now. Galvin and the others were expecting him back. He'd play out the game until later. He dug his hands into the earth of the steep side, used his feet against the boulder to push off, and began to slowly crawl up. Catching small, tough mountain weeds and digging in with his heels, he pulled himself along the almost vertical mountainside, not unlike some strange, giant insect making its way along. But he finally reached the incline and climbed over the edge. He rested for a moment and then pushed to his feet, avoided the silent forms that lay on the path, and hurried up to reach the top as dark fell.

Everyone rushed forward as he appeared, all anxious-faced, each holding to his or her own concerns.

"It worked," he bit out grimly, and quickly recounted how the big dray had thundered into the pursuers. "They're about done in," he finished, and his eyes went to Lottie.

She stared back but he saw the combination of relief and pain in her eyes.

"The wagon. What happened to the wagon?" Howard Galvin asked.

"It hit the wall. The front wheels buckled, but the rest is all right. We can try pulling it back in the morning," he said. "Now I'm going to get some sleep." He walked to the Ovaro, took his bedroll, and started to move to the rear of the table of rock when Janet caught up to him.

"What went wrong?" she asked, and he kept the surprise from his face only by waiting a second before he turned to her.

"What makes you think that?" He frowned.

"It was in your telling of it," Janet said. "No being pleased, no satisfaction, not the hint of a job well done."

Damn her acuteness, he swore inwardly. "I just told it the way it happened." He shrugged.

"Only there was something more," she said stubbornly.

"I'm tired, that's all," he said.

Her eyes told him she rejected the answer, but the

130

questioning left her face. "I'm glad you're back safe," she said softly.

"Concerned caring or self-interest?" he queried.

"Now who has a suspicious turn of mind?" she returned, and hurried away.

Fargo walked on, put down his bedroll, and stretched out but stayed clothed. He let the camp settle down, and when he was sure everyone else was asleep, he rose, left the pinto, and on steps silent as a mountain cat's stole from the camp. He hurried down the incline under a half-moon that afforded more than enough light. He spotted the soft, orange glow of a camp fire when he reached the bottom and moved toward it. He slowed when he saw the figure with a rifle standing at one side of the small fire. Peering past the figure, he saw four men around the fire and one more sentry facing in the opposite direction.

He moved forward and made no effort to be quiet.

The nearest sentry brought his rifle up as he went into a crouch. "Hold it there, whoever you are," the man called out, and the other figures around the fire snapped to life and Fargo caught the glint of a six-gun in every hand. "Come in with your hands up," the sentry ordered, and his arms raised, Fargo stepped into the light. He saw the man in the red-checked shirt on one knee, a big Remington .44 single-action in his hand. He also saw the star-shaped silver badge pinned to the front of his shirt. A square-faced man with graying hair and a ruddy complexion, a short nose, heavy eyebrows, Fargo noted.

"Who are you, mister?" the man asked.

"Name's Fargo. Skye Fargo. Some call me the Trailsman," Skye answered, and lowered his arms. The man's eyes searched his face.

"What are you doing here?" he questioned.

"Looking for some answers. You're wearing a sheriff's badge," Fargo said.

"So I am. Sheriff Ray Hogan of Fork Pass, Wyoming," the man said.

"You're a long way out of your territory, Sheriff," Fargo said.

"I am. How's that concern you?" Hogan asked.

"I don't know, not yet. I was hoping you might tell me," Fargo said.

The sheriff winced as he moved his leg. "What the hell is all this about, mister?" he barked.

"Maybe about Howard Galvin. You after him?" Fargo said, and saw the surprise slide across Hogan's face.

The man pushed himself to his feet with a grimace of pain. "What do you know about Howard Galvin?"

Fargo drew in a deep breath. "He's part of the wagon train I've been taking through the mountains," Fargo said, and saw a second wave of surprise flood the sheriff's face. He chose his next words carefully, unwilling to lie yet not willing to wallow in self-accusation. "I guess that makes me part of what just happened to you."

"Goddamn," Sheriff Hogan breathed. "How much a part?"

"Enough," Fargo said. "I'd no idea you were a sheriff's posse. We were already attacked by a pack of hired guns. I thought you were more of the same. When I heard one of your men call you sheriff, I decided to come down here on my own and get some answers."

"Why?" Hogan pressed.

"I don't like being played for a fool, taken in, and lied to, if that's what's been done," Fargo said.

"You just come to suspect that?" Sheriff Hogan asked.

"I figured I'd not been given the whole truth. It seems not from anyone on this damn trip. But I didn't know the law was involved," Fargo said.

Ray Hogan sank down to one knee again with another grimace of pain and lowered his Remington. "Sit down, Fargo," he said. "Yes, I'm after Howard Galvin."

"Why?" Fargo asked.

"Because he stole a hundred thousand dollars in gold from the Wyoming Gold Storage Company," the sheriff said. "That a good-enough reason?"

"It is. You sure of it?" Fargo questioned.

"Howard Galvin was bookkeeper for Wyoming Gold Storage for six years. Lottie Dill was his assistant. Wyoming Gold Storage was the main storage depot for the gold of a dozen mining companies. Galvin, with the help of his girlfriend, was siphoning gold from every shipment that came in and juggling the books to cover it up."

"What happened when a company called in its gold?"

"He paid it to them. There was always enough gold in storage and new shipments that came in once a month. He juggled the books and only he and his assistant knew the truth."

"Somebody found out, it seems," Fargo said.

"New owners came in. They decided to take a full inventory of all the gold on hand. Galvin knew the game was up. He resigned and took his assistant with him. Nobody suspected him then, not until the shortages were discovered. Of course, he not only resigned but disappeared."

"And they threw finding him to you," Fargo said.

"It was my territory," the sheriff said. "I had only one thing to go on. He had a hundred thousand in gold to move. You can't put that in a satchel. He went into hiding, but we kept looking and I put the word out far and wide. Wyoming Gold had already offered a reward for return of the gold."

"How'd you come onto him?" Fargo asked.

"I got word that a man fitting his description had bought three big heavy-haulage drays down on the Utah border," Hogan said. "That meant he was moving the gold. I knew if we found him and the wagons, we'd find the gold. Only it wasn't that easy. I had people all over looking for the three drays. At first I thought he'd head south, then maybe due north, but he didn't turn up anywhere. Then I finally heard that a man with three wagons had hired a pack of outriders and was headed for the Cabinet Mountains."

"It was easy to pick up our trail then," Fargo said.

"It still took time," Sheriff Hogan said. "And I'm still wondering where the hell Galvin was with the gold in the three months after he resigned."

"Now, what?" Fargo asked.

"You tell me. I can just about ride. I've only a few bruised men left. The rest are all dead and he's up there with a passel of hired guns, I'm sure. How many does he have?"

"Enough," Fargo grunted.

The sheriff swore bitterly. "All I need is him and the gold and I can take him in. We're healthy enough to do that much," the man said.

Fargo's thoughts whirled. Galvin had taken him for a royal carousel ride of deceit, trickery, and clever manipulation. The man was a big-time embezzler, a crook. He deserved to be brought in with his stolen gold. "Maybe I can help you," Fargo slid at the sheriff.

"Spell it out," Hogan said.

"The one wagon is halfway up the incline. Come dawn, you and your men walk to it. Hunker down behind it. Stay out of sight till I get there. I'll bring Galvin to you," Fargo said. "That's what you need, you said, him and the gold."

"Why, Fargo? Conscience?" the sheriff speared.

"That's a big part of it. I won't deny it," Fargo said.

"It's a deal. I'll be there if I have to crawl up," Hogan said.

"What about Lottie?" Fargo asked.

"Bring her," Hogan snapped.

"I got the feeling that anything she did was for Galvin," Fargo said. "He engineered everything."

"Doesn't matter. She was part of it. She can make her plea to a federal judge," Sheriff Hogan said.

Fargo nodded, unhappily. But the sheriff was right. And Lottie wasn't blameless. He'd given her more than one chance to tell him the truth, and each time she had backed away. "Tomorrow morning," he said, and started to turn away.

"The only reason I'm going along with you is that I've heard about you, Fargo," the sheriff said. "You've a straight reputation."

Fargo nodded and walked out of the small glow of light and into the darkness. He made his way up the incline, went into his mountain cat's walk when he neared the top, and slipped noiselessly into the sleeping campsite. He lay down on his bedroll and drew sleep to himself at once. He woke with the morning sun, rose, used his canteen to freshen up, and waited until the others stirred.

When Galvin emerged from his converted grocery wagon, Lottie behind him, Fargo sauntered over to the man. "Let's go down and have a look at your wagon," he said. Galvin nodded, started to call Hurd Bell when Fargo stopped him. "Just the three of us," he said. "I don't want too much noise and clatter. Can't say who might be listening below."

"That's right," Galvin said.

"Everybody relax till we get back," Fargo called to the others as he led the way down the incline. "Quietly," he muttered to Galvin as they made their way downward. Two could play games, he murmured inwardly.

As they drew closer to where the wagon lay against the wall, the bodies of the sheriff's men began to litter the incline and he saw Lottie keep her eyes staring straight ahead. He reached the wagon, halted, and saw Howard Galvin peer at the canvas covering.

"Everything's still in place," Galvin said, relief in his voice.

"Including us," Fargo heard Sheriff Hogan's voice cut in, and the man rose up from behind the wagon as

135

the other five of his men appeared from below and from the front end of the dray.

Howard Galvin's eyes went to Fargo at once. "What the hell is this?" he barked.

"This is Sheriff Ray Hogan of Wyoming," Fargo said. "You've been lying to me all along, you little weasel. You knew it was a sheriff's posse that might come after you."

"I don't know what you're talking about, Fargo," Galvin said.

"Drop it. The sheriff told me everything about you and the Wyoming Gold Storage Company," Fargo said.

"I didn't steal their damn gold," Galvin said almost offhandedly, and Fargo found himself unsettled by the man's cool brazenness.

"That's why you've been running with this secret cargo and your hired guards," Fargo said.

"I'm innocent," Howard insisted. "I resigned. The gold shortage was found and they put the rest together to blame me."

"Take the tarp off that wagon," the sheriff ordered. "We'll put an end to this bullshit."

"That's my wagon. It's private property. You've no right to touch it without a judge's order," Galvin protested.

"Open it," Hogan barked at his men, who had hesitated.

Fargo stood back as the sheriff's men took their knives and cut the ropes that crisscrossed the tarpaulin to seal it tight as a drumskin. The ropes fell away and the men ripped the tarpaulin from the wagon and Fargo found himself staring at a wagon filled with rocks, little rocks, medium rocks, fair-sized rocks. He exchanged glances with the sheriff. "The gold's underneath. He wouldn't put it on top," Sheriff Hogan said. "Turn the wagon over."

"Jesus, not this baby. She's too heavy," one of the men said. "Best we can do is get her on her side."

"That'll do," Hogan said.

Fargo stepped back as the men bent low under one side of the big dray, their shoulders against the bottom rim of the body. They lifted together. The wagon moved. They lifted again, dug in, lifted once more, and the big dray tipped over. It crashed on its side and the contents spilled out across the incline until the wagon was all but empty.

"Rocks," Fargo bit out. "Goddamn rocks. Nothing else."

8

"I'll be dammed," Ray Hogan said, awe in his voice. "I'll be dammed."

Fargo wrenched his own stare from the pile of rocks to shoot a glance at Lottie. She, too, stared at the emptied wagon with pure shock in her face, her lips parted in disbelief.

"Satisfied?" Howard Galvin asked, unable to hide the smirk of triumph in his voice.

Fargo's eyes stayed on Lottie as she turned from the pile of rocks to Howard. Her arm came up and lashed out, the slap a stinging, sharp sound as it smashed across Howie's face.

"Goddamn you, Howie. Goddamn you," she spit at him, spun on her heel, and strode off up the incline.

No act. No performance. Her shock and her fury were too real for that. It was plain that Lottie had expected something else in the wagon—the gold, no doubt. It fit, Fargo reflected. It explained some of the concerns she had voiced to him over Howard: "Howie will be too busy protecting the wagons to look out for himself," she had said. But Howie had really flung a breach of confidence at her, probably thinking he could get away with it. Galvin's voice broke into his thoughts.

"I'll be going on with my trip now, Sheriff," Howard said. "And I'll be sending you a bill for my wagon."

"Go to hell," Ray Hogan snapped, but Galvin returned a chiding smile as he turned to Fargo.

"As for you, Fargo, I'll expect an apology and that

you'll carry on our contract, even if you've proven to be something of a turncoat," Galvin said.

"I made a contract. I'll carry it out. Don't expect anything else," Fargo growled, and Galvin strode up the incline after Lottie.

"Wait a minute," the sheriff called out. "Maybe I want a look at those other two drays."

"Be my guest," Galvin said, and hurried on, the answer proof that there'd be nothing but more rocks in the other wagons.

"We just gonna let him walk away?" one of the sheriff's deputies frowned. "We ought to bring him back, anyway."

"I can't arrest a man for carrying rocks," Hogan answered bitterly. "I bring him back and the judge will throw me and the case out. No evidence, no gold, no case." He paused and grimaced in a combination of pain in his leg and utter frustration. "Why the hell would he do this? Why would he go to all the effort to haul three wagons of rocks across these mountains?"

"He went to all that trouble for you," Fargo said. "To make you hear about what he'd bought and the guards he'd hired. All to convince you he was moving the gold. All the time you waited for him to surface, then picked up his movements and followed us into the mountains, he was moving the gold another way. He made himself and his wagons into a giant red herring for you, Sheriff, and he expected you'd come chasing after him."

Sheriff Hogan stared at Fargo as the words stabbed through him. "Goddamn little bastard," the sheriff murmured finally. "Now he goes on, with you taking him the rest of the way, and we bury our dead and limp home."

"You could keep on shadowing us," Fargo said.

"No, I'm too bruised for it. So's everybody else," the sheriff said. "Besides, I'm out of my territory now, way out. I don't know as I could legitimately operate in Washington Territory." He paused, stared into space

139

for a long moment, and then brought his eyes back to the big man in front of him. "Maybe there is one way to stop the bastard," Ray Hogan said. "You."

"Me?" Fargo frowned.

"You're taking him someplace. If what you say is right, he aims to meet up with that gold he's had sent some other way. If you could nail him with just one bag, that'd be enough. Bring him and the bag back and Wyoming Storage will figure a way to pick up the rest and give you a mighty handsome reward," the sheriff said, his voice growing excited.

Fargo felt his own excitement rising as he listened. It would help settle scores with Howard Galvin. It'd make up for being tricked. It would be an offering, though pitifully inadequate, to those he'd been duped into helping to slay. "It's a deal. I'll do it. I'll nail the clever little bastard," Fargo said.

"Good," Ray Hogan said. "We'll clean up here, put the dead on their mounts, and bury them someplace else. Then I'll go back to Fork Pass and wait. It may take you a while, but I'm a patient man."

Fargo nodded, his lips a thin line, and began to climb to the top of the incline. He reached it to find Howard Galvin in the driver's seat, a quiet smugness in his round face. Lottie, holding herself very stiff, sat beside him and stared straight ahead.

"Can we roll?" Galvin asked with a trace of testiness, and Fargo climbed onto the Ovaro. Ginny and Gwen were driving and he saw Janet on the gray mare.

"Take lead wagon," he said to Ginny as he moved from the rock table and started down the incline. When he reached the bottom, he turned west again along the narrow cut of land as Janet came up to him.

"May I ride with you?" she asked. "I'd like to know what happened back there."

"What'd Galvin say?" he asked.

"Only that he lost one dray and the men had fled," she answered.

Fargo made a wry sound, sent the Ovaro into a canter, and rode away from the others with Janet at his heels. He finally slowed where the cut ended, and he scanned the mountains for another pass. He found a wide swath where lightning had once struck and burned away at least five miles of forest. Janet's eyes questioned and he decided to tell her most of it. When he finished, her face reflected surprise and a frown of curiosity.

"That's quite a story," she said. "Makes my lies sound small-time."

"Don't be too proud of yourself," he said, and she looked instantly contrite.

"I'm not," she said. "I did what I had to do. I'm not proud of it." Her snapping blue eyes had grown soft and suddenly she seemed terribly tired and somehow all the more attractive for it.

Fargo felt sorry for her. She'd gotten into something she couldn't handle from the outset, mainly two curvaceous, throbbing volcanoes.

"Sorry, didn't mean to push at you," he said, and her quick smile brightened her face.

"What happens now?" she asked.

"I finish my job."

"And Howard Galvin gets away with everything."

"Seems that way."

"Why don't I believe you?" Janet asked. "Why don't I believe you're going to stand by and let that happen?"

Her sharpness again, he thought. "Maybe it's that suspicious nature of yours again." He smiled.

"It's my having come to know more about you," she said, and fell silent for a moment. "I feel sorry for Lottie," she said suddenly.

"Why?"

"She was with him all the way. Yet he didn't have enough confidence in her to tell her about the rocks."

"Maybe he didn't have enough confidence in her acting ability," Fargo said.

"You're being kind to him."

"Doesn't much matter. We'll be out of the mountains tomorrow. Another day and you'll be at the mission school. What happens to Janet Johnson, then?"

"I find a stage south. There must be one from Colfax. Then I take another someplace and another and another until I've gone all the way down and around back to Gannon City. I write to Simon then and tell him the job is done," she said. "But first, I take a few days' rest before traveling again. I understand there's an inn in Colfax. Why don't you come visit me?"

"I'll try," he said.

"Which means if you're not on Howard Galvin's tail," she said.

"Don't be smart," he growled.

Her hand reached out and covered his where it rested on the saddle horn. "I'm sorry we couldn't get to know each other better. You're an infuriating and very wonderful man," she said. "I'm very much in your debt."

"That's quite a speech for you," he said.

"Yes, I'm just not good at putting what I feel into words," she said.

"Only some things," he said. "I seem to remember you're damn good at putting anger into words. And actions."

She shrugged, sheepishness coming over her. "You're right. It's only some things I've trouble with," she said, and drew her hand back as the others came into sight. She returned to Gwen and Ginny.

Fargo waved the wagons onto the burned-out, wide swatch of land. Except for picking their way around charred tree stumps, they made good time, and when night came, the land had begun to descend. Everyone ate in silence, and when he finished, Fargo found Ginny and Gwen at his side.

"Where are you going to be later?" Gwen asked.

"Asleep. And so are you," he said firmly, and they frowned.

"We never figured you to turn down an offer," Ginny said.

"I'm making an exception," he said. "You two have to learn you can't always have your way."

He saw their eyes narrow. "We like to get our way," Gwen said. "What if we told Janet you slept with us?"

Fargo stared back at them for a moment of disbelief and then let a smile cross his face. "Major mistake, honey. I'm not Tom Bailey. I don't give a shit who you tell what. Now, get out of my sight before I take your britches down for another reason."

Both their faces tightened and they turned as one and hurried to the wagon.

He had to shift his opinion of them, he realized. They were still not predatory, but they wrapped sex in their uncaring arrogance and had no qualms about hurting others to get their way. A few years at the mission school was very much what they needed, he thought as he took his bedroll a dozen yards away and stretched out. He was starting to go to sleep when he saw the figure in the robe moving toward him, and he sat up.

Lottie halted, a tiredness in her round face. Even her tight blond curls seemed to have lost some of their firmness. "I suppose there's nothing I can say," she murmured.

"You had your chance," he said.

"It's not as though he stole from people, poor people, took their money or possessions. It's a big company," she said.

"You defending him or yourself?" Fargo rasped.

"I'm trying to explain."

"You can't," he said harshly.

She half-shrugged. "Thank you, anyway," she said, and he frowned back. "For taking us on through the rest of the way. For carrying on your part of it."

143

"It was a contract. I gave my word on it. Don't thank me," he said.

"Most men would've figured Howie broke it and gone their way."

"I'm not most men," he told her, and she nodded gravely, turned, and slowly walked away, a woman aware of right and wrong while trapped in her own loyalties. The strands of the past that never leave, he reflected as he lay down and drew sleep to himself.

He rose with the morning and called an early start. The passes grew more plentiful, most moving downhill as they descended from the tall peaks. By the day's end they were in the foothills, and the flatland of the Kamiak Butte stretched in the distance. He went off by himself and everyone slept quickly. He had set a long day and a hard pace.

In the morning, he did the same and they rolled quickly across the butte. It was a little past the noon hour when they crossed into Washington Territory, a cracked wooden sign stuck in the dirt proclaiming the fact.

"Colfax is dead ahead, I'd guess," Fargo said as he drew to a halt.

"We'll make it fine from here," Galvin said with a wide smile. "You're all paid up, Fargo. We've nothing more to settle."

Fargo's reply stayed inside himself and he returned Hurd Bell's friendly wave. He and his men were probably the only true innocents on the entire trip, strangely enough. They never really knew half of what had gone on or that they were part of the picture Howard Galvin had so carefully painted for Sheriff Hogan. Lottie offered a wave as Galvin sent the wagon forward, and he allowed a nod and then Janet was rolling up alongside him, the girls beside her.

"Try to come visit at the inn," she said brightly. It was obvious that Gwen and Ginny had said nothing to her. Once they realized their threats had no power over him, they had no excuse to use them. Both stared straight ahead sullenly, he noted. "The mission school is some ten miles south of Colfax," Janet said. "I'll be going there first." She paused and turned to the girls. "Aren't you going to say good-bye to Fargo?" she asked. "Where are your manners?"

"We already did," Ginny said, her tone surly.

"What's wrong with you two this morning?" Janet asked them.

"Can we please get going?" Gwen snapped, and Janet offered Fargo an apologetic shrug.

He tossed her a smile as she sent the team forward. He waited till she and Galvin were out of sight and then put the pinto into a fast canter. He made a wide circle and was in Colfax before Galvin arrived. He rode down the main street, much the same as that in every other town, with perhaps a few more basket phaetons and surreys than might be found in some. There apparently were some people of substance in and around Colfax.

A long-bodied, three-seat platform wagon with a canopy top caught his eye and he saw the words ANGEL MISSION SCHOOL painted along the side. An elderly man sat with the reins in hand, and as Fargo watched, six nuns emerged from a general store with packages and climbed into the wagon.

He rode on, passed the Colfax Inn, a two-story wood-frame structure neatly painted with three hitching posts in the rear. But his eyes sought other places and he found the first near the end of town, a big, weathered building with a sign STORAGE AND WAREHOUSE over the double doors. He circled the building before he rode on to halt again at a somewhat smaller structure with the words FREIGHT DEPOT across the door. He circled the building also and made mental notes of a side door and two windows. He went on to the end of town to make certain those were the only two buildings of their kind. The freight depot would clearly hold shipments recently arrived or soon to go. The other would handle long-term storage. Either could hold the key to what he sought. Howard Galvin had not come to Colfax on a whim. The gold he had moved some other way was either here or soon would be.

Fargo continued out of town and circled Colfax as he wound his way back the way he had come. He'd play a waiting game first. Maybe that would be enough. A weasel knows where it has stored its food.

He saw a hillock of bur oak and sent the Ovaro toward it. He dismounted and stretched out in the warm afternoon sun. He catnapped and finally rose to climb into the saddle when the sun began to nod toward the horizon line. He hadn't decided about visiting Janet at the inn, but now it seemed perhaps a convenient way to keep an eye on the town at the same time. He rode back into town and reined up at the inn, where, inside the front door, a desk clerk in a green eyeshade greeted him from behind a Dutch door.

"Looking for Miss Janet Johnson," Fargo said.

The man, middle-aged and balding, frowned in thought. "Nobody registered here by that name," he said.

"Young woman, attractive, dark-brown hair. She'd have checked in sometime during the last few hours," Fargo said.

"No, sir. I've been here all day," the man said.

Fargo felt the furrow push into his brow. She'd had more than enough time to deposit the girls and return to Colfax. Perhaps she'd run into unexpected admission problems. Or something else, he bit out silently, remembering what the man had told him about Iris Bailey. Apprehension growing inside him, he ran from the inn, vaulted onto the Ovaro, and set off at a gallop for the mission school.

The building finally materialized, tall, with a cross-topped bell tower and high concrete walls. Two nuns came out when he reined to a halt.

"Can we help you?" one inquired. "I'm Sister Marie."

"I'm looking for Janet Johnson. She was to bring

two young ladies to you today. She was on her way here when I left her," Fargo said.

"Yes, Ginny and Gwen Simon. We were notified by post they'd be arriving. But Miss Johnson hasn't appeared today," the nun said.

Fargo bit off the curse that formed in his throat. "Thanks. I'll be coming back," he said, and sent the Ovaro into a gallop. He returned to where he'd left Janet and followed the wagon tracks. She had gone south toward the mission school for at least a half-hour. The tracks formed a straight line, but suddenly turned. He glanced up to see a small hill densely covered with bur oak and box elder. He followed, one hand on the hip of the big Colt at his side as he reached the dense tree cover. He slowed, edged his way into the trees where the wagon tracks had squeezed through an opening. He halted, let his eyes grow accustomed to the dimness of the dense forest, when he saw the square bulk of Janet's wagon wedged in between two trees.

Lips pulled back in apprehension, the Colt in hand, he dismounted and crept toward the silent wagon. The rear canvas flap hung open and he saw the form, facedown, on the floor of the wagon. He swung inside, dropped to one knee, and turned the figure over to see Janet, a bandanna across her mouth, but her eyes open and awake. He noted the ropes that bound her wrists and ankles. He took the bandanna off first, then drew his knife to cut her bonds. "Iris Bailey?" he asked.

"No, not Iris Bailey. Gwen and Ginny, those rotten little bitches," Janet snapped as she sat up. "They jumped me, knocked me down, and tied me up. They said they weren't going to any damn mission school. Then they drove the wagon in here."

Fargo helped her from the rear of the wagon as she rubbed her wrists. "They took the team of horses and rode off," she said. "I don't know where they think they're going."

"With their attitudes and their talents, they'll find someplace," Fargo said. "But if you don't deliver them to the school, you don't collect from their father, right?" She nodded and Fargo heard a sound from inside the forest. His Colt was raised instantly and then he saw the gray mare a few yards away. He felt a pressure against his chest and Janet was leaning there.

"Thank God you found me. I could've stayed there without ever being found. I could've died in there," she said. "What made you come looking for me?"

"You hadn't shown up at the inn or at the mission," he said, and she clung to him a moment longer. "Take the gray mare and go back to the mission," he said.

"What are you going to do?" she asked.

"Go quail-hunting," he said, and waited while she took the mare and rode from the forested hill. He surveyed the ground and quickly picked up the two sets of hoofprints that led north. They had the sense not to go to Colfax, not right away. Perhaps they'd wind up there, but they were putting distance between themselves and the town and the school. The prints were simple as a first-grade primer to follow as they rode side by side. They weren't expecting to be followed, of course, he realized, and he slowed when the hoofprints turned into a dip of land and he saw the glitter of a mountain stream in the last of the sun. He drifted into a line of hackberry until he saw the two figures, both dismounted, refreshing themselves at the stream, both as lusciously lovely as ever.

And as self-centered, he added silently as he took his lariat and dismounted. He stole closer on noiseless steps, not that they'd have picked up ordinary footsteps. They were too busy chattering. He chose Gwen. She was closest. He lifted the lariat, gave it one fast twirl, and sent it sailing through the air. It landed atop the girl, fell to her breasts to pin her arms at her sides. He yanked hard as he tightened the rope and she left her feet with a yelp.

Ginny, staring, just began to recover from her surprise when he was racing into the clear with the other end of the lariat. He swung it around her with one quick motion and yanked again, and she went down on her knees beside Gwen. He circled her with one more turn of the rope, this time letting the lariat go around Gwen, too.

He stepped back as they glared at him, initial surprise turning into icy anger. "Get up," he said, and they struggled to their feet together. "School's waiting."

"Fargo, listen to me," Ginny began. "You let us go and we'll give you a month you'll never forget."

"I'm never going to forget this one as it is," Fargo said, and pulled them along as he returned to the Ovaro. He swung into the saddle, allowed enough slack in the lariat for them to walk side by side, and began to move from the dip of land. He saw the two team horses amble after him as he turned south.

"You can't do this. You can't make us walk all the way back," Ginny protested.

"Watch," he said.

"We'll be too tired to breathe," Gwen said.

"That's the idea. You'll be nice and quiet for a week while you get used to the place," Fargo said. He set a slow pace, held the Ovaro to a walk, and listened to Gwen and Ginny moan and groan with increasing despair as each minute passed.

Night fell and he halted as they stumbled, got up, stumbled again and rose once more. They cursed at him in between groans of real pain now.

"Bastard. You've no right to do this," Ginny gasped out.

"Penitence. Anybody can administer it," he said, and pulled them along.

The tall tower of the Angel Mission School finally took shape, and when he reached the door, three nuns hurried out and he saw Janet follow. She paused to shoot Gwen and Ginny a bitter glance before she turned to Fargo.

"I told the sisters what happened," she said as he

loosened the lariat around the girls enough for the nuns to remove.

"You've my sympathy, Sisters," he said as he gathered in his lariat.

"We are quite used to difficult applicants here," Sister Marie said, and he watched Gwen and Ginny painfully take halting steps into the school with two of the sisters.

"Can you use two good team horses, Sister?" he asked with a nod to the two steeds that had halted.

"Indeed we can. I'll send one of the men out for them, and thank you," the nun said.

"Get the gray mare," Fargo said to Janet, and she hurried inside the walls to reappear in moments atop the horse. The door of the school closed and Janet met his eyes. "I'll take you to town," he said. "You can get your things from the wagon in the morning."

"All right," she said, and swung in beside him. "Seems I have to say thank you again," she remarked.

"You don't have to," he said.

"I do have to, and I want to," Janet said. "Fact is, I've run out of words to say it."

"You'll think of something," he said, and put the pinto into a trot until they reached Colfax, mostly darkened now except for the glow of light from the dance hall.

A lamp burned outside the door of the inn and an older man sat behind the small Dutch door now.

"Be right back," Fargo said as Janet registered for a room. He went to the rear of the inn and smiled as he saw the two big drays unhitched to one side. It was what he expected. Galvin felt safe. He had won. He'd no reason to make hurried mistakes now.

Fargo had seen a public stable earlier in his ride through town and he took the Ovaro there, got him a roomy corner stall, and returned to the hotel.

"Room Four, end of hallway," the man said.

Fargo found the room and Janet opened to his knock. Her face was bright, still with little droplets of water on it where she had freshened up from the big porcelain basin in the room. It was a small room, mostly taken up by a big double bed and the dresser against one wall.

"I should be exhausted," Janet said. "But I'm wide awake. I guess everything that's happened has yet to wear off."

"It takes a while," he said.

She brushed her hair back with one hand. "Are you staying at the inn tonight?"

"That depends," he said, and she raised an eyebrow. "On if I get an invitation," he finished. His lake-blue eyes were steady on her and she looked away.

"I don't know," she murmured huskily.

"You don't know what?"

"Whether it'd be right. Whether I ought to," she said.

"Do you want me to stay?" he asked firmly but softly.

"Yes," Janet murmured, still looking away.

He took her chin in his hand and turned her face toward him. "I didn't hear that," he said.

"Yes, dammit, you heard it. Yes," she said, a surge of wildness coming into her voice, and suddenly her arms were locked around his neck, her lips pressed hard against his. He responded, let his tongue dart out, and she uttered a tiny half-scream.

"No, I don't know," she said, but her arms stayed locked around his neck. They were but inches from the bed and he pushed gently and she went down. His hand moved under the white shirt and closed around a modest, very soft mound. "No, oh, no . . . oh, God," Janet cried out as she tried to twist away from him. He drew his hand back and she grew still except for her deep breaths.

He opened the buttons of the shirt as his mouth pressed hers and she kissed him back with short, almost frantic bursts of wanting wrapped in self-discipline.

The shirt fell open and he took in modest breasts but with a lovely upturned line to them, a soft sweep of the underside of the cup that crested at the pink, firm nipples. She lay still again, her eyes on him, almost frightened, watching as he looked at her. Gently, he brought his lips down to one very pink nipple on a light-pink areola, pressed, drew the tip into the moistness between his lips.

"Oh, oh, oooooh, God," Janet cried out, and her back arched. Her hips twisted, but her hands came up to lock behind his neck. She twisted again and her shirt came off and he saw nice round shoulders, a lean torso, and a narrow waist. His hand pulled the waist button of her skirt open, pushed, and her half-slip came down with it and he saw lean, long legs yet nicely turned, long calves with just enough flesh on them to give shape, and a flat abdomen with a small but dense little nap beneath.

He pulled back, let her lie alone, and she seemed almost rigid as he pulled off clothes. But her snapping blue eyes were bright as she watched him undress, followed the line of his muscled frame to his already rising maleness. She seemed in a trance, eyes fixed on him. It wasn't until he brought his body down against hers that the trance snapped. Their skins touched, warmth against warmth, tingling flesh touching, taking on new sensations with the contact. His mouth found one upturned breast again, and this time he drew in more of it and felt Janet's hands tighten around his neck. "Oh, oh, my God . . . oh, nice . . . nice . . . Oh, God, nice . . ." she murmured, and as he stroked and caressed with hands and lips, moved up and down her body, her short cries grew longer, became high-pitched moans.

His fingers pushed through the dense, little black nap, rested on the Venus mound beneath, and then slid downward. He felt her body tighten at once, resist, and he paused, waiting until she relaxed. When she did, he stayed, unmoving until he felt her hips lift, the body offering its own invitation, and his fingers slipped into the dark, secret place. He touched and Janet screamed, drew her legs together, screamed again, and then let her lean legs fall apart. He explored, gently, her smooth softness. Only after he did so, did he feel her response, moist heat joining the smooth linings, and he heard her moaning. Her legs opened and closed, almost meaninglessly, as though she didn't know what to do with them. He moved, brought his erect, throbbing warmth against her, and her body bucked upward in a sudden spasm of sensation. He slid forward slowly, and her legs found their place as they came up and clasped against his sides.

She was moaning and there was both denial and demand in each wail. He moved slowly inside her and felt her relax. Soon her lean body moved with his, thrusting forward, drawing back, and pushing to embrace him again in its soft walls. "Yes, yes, oh, nice . . . so nice, so good, oh, God, yes," Janet murmured, words a litany of pleasure that, when they finally quickened, became a gasped, breathy sound and he felt her hands digging into his back. "My God, oh, my God," Janet screamed. "It . . . it's happening. Oh, God, now, now. Oh, oh." Her legs drew up, knees reached his ribs, and she seemed rolled up in a strange little ball as she quivered and screamed and shook. His mouth held one upswept breast deeply as he exploded with her and there were no screams from her suddenly, only a frantic hissing sound as she thrust against him, knees drawn up, crotch tight to his, as though she were trying to exchange bodies.

But finally she ceased hissing and he felt her go limp. Her knees slid down from his side and she fell back on the bed, her eyes staring at him with a strangeness, almost as though she disbelieved what had happened. He stayed with her, and the strange expression finally faded from her eyes as her arms came around his shoulders. "From the very first," she murmured.

"Very first what?" he asked.

"From the very first day I came onto you near naked in the sun," she said. "I've been wondering ever since. Wanting, I guess, though never letting myself admit it." He moved to lay beside her lean loveliness and she wore an almost shy little smile. "I didn't want you to think I was like Ginny and Gwen," she said.

"You're not," he told her.

She stretched in lean beauty, one arm around his neck. "You know, I'm so glad I interrupted Gwen with you that night," she said. "God knows what might have happened. They're both apparently very powerful. Of course, I wouldn't be here if I thought you'd made love to her that night."

"I didn't." He smiled. "You know that."

"Yes," she said. "And now I'm really glad for that."

"Me, too," he murmured. It wasn't a lie. Not exactly.

She curled up against him, one upturned breast into his chest, and was asleep in minutes.

He felt the weariness of the day sweeping over him, also, and he closed his eyes, cradled her in his arms, and slept soundly till morning woke him.

She sat up, rubbed sleep from her eyes, and looked as lovely as a morning glory. "There's a bathroom down the hall," she said, swinging from the bed and drawing on her shirt and skirt.

"Ladies first," he said, and lay back as she left the room. One name immediately rose in his mind: Howard Galvin. Right now, the man didn't know he was in Colfax. He'd keep it that way awhile longer, Fargo decided. When Janet returned, he went to the bathroom, washed, and dressed.

She was waiting by the door when he came in.

"Shall we go get my things in the wagon?" she asked.

"Later. I've some other things to do first," he said.

"Such as finding Howard Galvin?" she asked, a tiny smile in her eyes.

"I want to make sure he's in town still," Fargo said,

and slipped from the room. He hurried down the corridor, found a rear door to the inn with a small window that let him see to the hitching area in the rear. The two big drays were still there, but there were two men beside them, one in overalls and a torn shirt. He almost didn't recognize the other one, either, as he saw a short, roundish figure in a gray frock coat with matching trousers, a wing collar, and a blue cravat with diamond stickpin. He also carried a walking stick he used with jaunty aplomb as he spoke.

"Goddamn," Fargo breathed. "It's Galvin." He stared again at the impeccably dressed figure, only the round, puffy face and thinning hair the same.

"The rocks you can throw away, my good man, but the drays will bring you a good price. They've only been used on one trip," he heard Howard say.

"All right, it's a deal, mister. I'll send a boy from my place to pick them up," the other man said, and trudged away.

Fargo watched Howard motion in the air, and from alongside the inn, a beautiful, deep-blue Victoria drove up, the woman at the reins in a deep-blue silk dress with a white collar and puffed sleeves. She wore a large, fancy, go-to-meeting hat, but he glimpsed the tight blond curls peeking out from under it.

"Lottie, by God," Fargo breathed, and watched Howard step into the carriage beside her. The carriage made a wide circle to leave, but Fargo was already racing down the corridor to the front door. Janet stepped outside as he passed, a frown on her face. "Stay there. I'll be back," he said as he dashed on and halted at the front of the inn, dropped to one knee behind a low hedge, and watched the carriage drive up the main street. He peered after it and saw it halt in front of the Colfax Bank. Lottie went into the bank with Howard, and Fargo felt Janet behind him. "I told you to stay put," he said.

"What's going on?" she asked, ignoring his remark.

"Howard and Lottie, dressed in the finest duds in a

fancy carriage. They just went into the bank," he said, and Janet knelt down beside him. He guessed it was some fifteen minutes when Howard and Lottie emerged from the bank. Galvin carried two small bank sacks. They got into the carriage and Lottie drove away through town.

"What do you make of it?" Janet asked.

"I don't know yet. Let's go ask some questions," he said, rose, and strode toward the bank with Janet hurrying to keep up with him. He entered the bank and saw only a few depositors at the lone window. He walked past to where a man in a brown suit rose from behind a desk.

"May I help you?" the man said. "I'm Roger Chasen, president of the Colfax Bank."

"Came here to meet Howard Galvin. Has he been here yet?" Fargo asked.

"Howard Galvin? I'm afraid I don't know any such person," the man said.

"Somebody told me they just saw him leave. Short man in a gray frock coat and cravat with a diamond stickpin," Fargo said.

"That's not Howard Galvin. That's Henry Gaylord," the bank president said.

"Henry Gaylord?" Fargo frowned.

"Oh, yes. He's a very wealthy man from California, I believe. He's been sending us deposits by mail for over six years now, one a month," Roger Chasen said.

"A deposit a month for six years. And you just keep on taking them," Fargo said.

"Well, it's not exactly that way. Mr. Gaylord and his wife were here six years ago. He established his account with us, purchased a house, and told us he might not be returning to live here for some years. But he told us he'd be sending a deposit of gold once a month through the mails, and that's what he's done like clockwork," the banker said.

"It must have reached a sizable amount now," Fargo said.

"Indeed, but now Mr. Gaylord is here to live, he tells me," Chasen said. "However, this Howard Galvin is not anyone I've ever heard. Certainly he's not one of our depositors."

"Maybe I was given the wrong name. Gaylord's wife, her name Lottie?" Fargo queried.

"In fact, it is," the man said.

"Where do they live. I think I have to clear this up," Fargo said.

"West of town about two miles, on Chasm Road. You'll see the sign. You'll see the chasm, too. It runs into a forest of hackberry near their house, a deep cut in the earth over two hundred feet down," Chasen said.

"Much obliged." Fargo smiled and left the bank with Janet clinging to his arm. "That's how the little weasel did it," he said to her as they reached the street. "He set it all up, sent a gold pouch each month so that when the time came, he wouldn't have to find a way to move all that gold."

"I guess he figured the time would come sooner or later," Janet said.

"He was smart enough to know that. Then he had to make it seem as though he were moving the gold. He'd already been accused of embezzling it. He knew they'd want to catch him with it. He also knew that if they caught him with nothing but rocks, their case would go out the window."

"So he set up the giant red herring you spoke about," Janet said.

"Yes, but not exactly for the reasons I thought. He wasn't moving the gold some other way at the same time. But with one stroke, he sent them on a wild-goose chase that, if they caught him, would blow their case away."

"Which is just what happened," Janet said.

"Not yet," Fargo said. "All I need is to bring him back with one bag, Hogan said. And we saw him leave the bank with two." He halted in front of the stable and Janet waited. "Go back to the inn, get the mare, and go get your stuff from the wagon. I'll finish this."

"Let me come along. You might need help," she said.

"With Galvin and Lottie? I don't think so, honey," he said. "But thanks. You just wait till I get back."

She walked on, not looking terribly happy, and he went into the stable, paid the fee, and saddled the Ovaro. He rode through town, followed the banker's instructions, and found Chasm Road. He halted as he saw the forest into which the deep chasm disappeared. The house, modest in size, rested against the edge of the forest, and he turned the horse and circled into the forest from the rear. When he reached the house, he saw the Victoria drawn up at one side and he slid to the ground and approached the house on silent steps.

He saw a rear door, tried the knob, and the door opened. He slipped into the house. A hallway beckoned in front of him and he heard Galvin's voice from the other end.

"Have you unpacked yet, Lottie?" Galvin called.

"Not yet," she said from another room.

Fargo crept along the hallway and came to a living room, sparsely furnished. Galvin sat at a small table, the two bank sacks beside him as he wrote into a ledger.

Fargo stepped into the room, the Colt in his hand. "The best-laid plans, Howie," he said, and saw Galvin look up, shocked horror flooding his puffy face.

His lips twitched before any sound came from them. "Fargo. What are you doing here?" he finally managed.

"Unfinished business," Fargo said. "I told you I don't like being taken."

"Look, Fargo, there's plenty of gold to split. There's no need to do anything you'll regret later when you think about it," Galvin said.

"I'm not going to. I'm going to do something you'll regret. Take you back," Fargo said.

"No," the voice cut in, and he half-turned to see

Lottie, a big over-and-under shotgun in her hands. "Dammit, Howie, I told you we should lay low. I told you he hadn't just walked away."

Fargo eyed the gun. It was steady, aimed directly at his stomach, much too close to miss.

"Drop the pistol, Fargo," Lottie said, and he let the Colt slide from his fingers to fall onto the floor.

"Shoot him," Galvin shouted.

"Here? Then, what? How do we get rid of him?" Lottie asked.

"Especially since I paid a visit to the bank. I'm sure they'll remember me," Fargo said.

"We'll tell them he came to hold us up," Galvin said.

Fargo glanced at Lottie and saw her lick her lips. She blinked, and the uncertainty stayed in her face. "Thanks," he said, and she flicked a glance at him. "For hesitating," he said.

"Goddammit, give me the gun," Galvin yelled, and charged toward her.

Fargo stuck his foot out and Galvin tripped on it. Never a well-balanced figure, he fell forward into Lottie. She tried to pull the gun out of the way, but it went off, the double explosion a shattering sound in the room. Fargo scooped up the Colt as Howard Galvin let out a guttural scream of pain and fell against the wall, half-turned, and slid to the floor, his midsection a gaping hole of red.

Lottie screamed, dropped the gun, and threw herself on him. "Oh, God, God. I didn't mean to do that. Oh, Howie, Howie," she said, and words became sobs that racked her body. She lay over him.

Fargo holstered the Colt and stepped to the window. The irises were coming into bloom, he noticed. He turned back only when Lottie's racking sobs had ceased and she lay against Galvin's lifeless form, her head on his shoulder.

He lifted her to her feet, led her from the room into an adjoining bedroom, where she sank down on the bed. "Wrong things end wrong," he said, not ungently.

Her tear-filled eyes stared at him. "What, now?"

"First, you go to town and report how Howie shot himself by accident," he said. "Then you stay awhile and be the grieving widow."

"Then, what?" she asked, rubbing her eyes dry. "You'll take me back instead of Howie?"

"Depends," he said. "Can you draw the gold from the bank?"

"No," she said. "Only Howie. He never could trust anybody completely."

"Yes, I remember," Fargo said, and Lottie gave him a wry glance. "That still leaves you with two bags of gold in the other room, more money than most folks see in a lifetime."

"What are you saying?"

"I'm saying take it and run, find a new life for yourself. You never had the guts of it. It was all Howie. You were a tool. The courts wouldn't see it that way, but that's the real truth of it. I'll report to Hogan, and the Wyoming Gold Storage people will send their lawyers to get their gold from the bank. But that'll all take months. You'll have time to gather yourself and take off when you're ready."

"Why are you doing this for me, Fargo?" she asked.

"I told you, you never were a real part of it. You did everything for Howie," he said.

"That's not enough. Why are you doing this for me?"

"Because you hesitated back there," he said. "And I knew then you were never going to pull that trigger." He took a step forward, pressed one big hand on the tight blond curls. "Find a new life," he said. "A second chance. That's damn hard to come by."

He started to turn and her hand caught at his. "I'm sorry for everything," she said. "And suddenly I'm most sorry I never made love to you."

"Who knows? Another day, another place," he said, and she let his hand drop. He strode from the house, took a deep breath of the fresh air outside, and re-trieved the Ovaro.

Janet was waiting outside the inn when he reached it.

"It'll take some telling," he said. "But it's over. Let's get your things from the wagon."

"And then?"

"You tell me," Fargo said.

"I want to go back with you," she said.

"You have a good reason?" he slid at her.

"I don't like stagecoaches."

"Smart-ass answer," he grunted.

"Smart-ass question," she snapped.

"We'll cut back through the mountains. It'll be shorter and easier with just the two of us," he said.

"And we can make love every night and I can discover all the things I only began to discover last night," she said.

"Now that's a reason," he said as her hand clasped his.

LOOKING FORWARD!
The following is the opening section
from the next novel in the exciting
Trailsman series from Signet:
THE TRAILSMAN #111
BLOOD CANYON

Summer, 1860, in western Utah Territory,
beyond the Humboldt Sink,
where liars, deceivers, fast guns, and Paiute
met for a last showdown . . .

Although he rode easy in the saddle, the big man
astride the magnificent black-and-white pinto stallion
trusted his sixth sense that always warned him of im-
pending danger: the Cheyenne were close. Too damn
close. As he listened to the sounds of nature, his
lake-blue eyes scanned the dense ground cover and
the whispering pines for the slightest sign to betray
their presence.

Moving the Ovaro north at a slow, cautious walk,
he followed the eastern contour at the base of the
Rocky Mountains. High above him, South Pass straddled the erratic Continental Divide. He knew the pass
well, had been on it many times. He glanced through
the canopy and squinted against bright sun rays
ricocheting off the mountaintop.

South Pass stood in the middle of Shoshoni Chief
Washakie's territory. But he knew there were no Sho-

shoni around at this time of year. Washakie had led them north on the Wind River Range. By now they were camped somewhere on the eastern banks of Jackson Lake.

The Cheyenne watched Washakie's movements. They always encroached on his territory the instant the Shoshoni struck their tepees and left their winter camp. Therefore, the big man knew he would find the Cheyenne encampment somewhere near the eastern slopes of the Rocky Mountains. He hoped he could get into their camp, do what he had to do, then work his way back out of it, all without being seen.

Suddenly the birds on his left stopped warbling. The Trailsman immediately reined to a halt. Easing his Sharps from its saddle case, he scanned in that area. He felt sure warriors were hiding in the outcrop of huge, jagged-edged rocks he saw.

A twig snapped on his right. So slight was the sound that only the Trailsman's wild-creature hearing would have noticed and known it was unnatural. He shifted his gaze to his right and saw nothing but pine towering out the thick undergrowth.

Then all hell broke loose. War-whooping Cheyenne braves sprung from the ground cover and from behind trees. They descended on him with their knives and hatchets held high as other Cheyenne poured out the outcrop. Half-naked warriors were all around him, too many to kill. Digging his boot heels into the Ovaro's flanks, he shot and dropped two of the screaming savages who were in front of the horse, trying to grab the bridle.

The stallion snorted a protest, reared and pawed the air. Hands grabbed the big man while others wrenched the deadly rifle from his grip. They pulled him to the ground and quickly relieved him of his big Colt. Other hands used his throwing rope to lash the big man's hands and powerful arms to his body. The free end of the rope was secured to his saddle horn.

A tall warrior leapt into the saddle and dug the heels of his moccasins into the Ovaro's flanks. The rope grew taut. Fists struck him as the Fargo started trotting. A warrior stuck out a foot and tripped him. He stumbled and fell facedown, tried to get up. They shoved him back down and told the rider dragging him to go faster. The big man's muscular body swiveled on the rope as it dragged him over rocks and through weeds. Low-hanging branches and barbed thickets tore at him, ripped his clothing, and scratched his chiseled face.

He was barely conscious when the rider reined the Ovaro to a halt. Fargo's ears buzzed. His bloody mouth and nostrils were clogged with dirt and dust. His eyes fluttered open. Looking out the corners of them, he brought a pair of much-worn moccasins into focus. He'd seen these moccasins before. The buzzing in his hearing ceased. He took a deep breath, closed his mouth, and exhaled through his nose. The mighty gush cleared it instantly of bloody dirt. He rolled onto his back and looked up at the man wearing the moccasins.

The man squatted and in good English said, "Skye Fargo, I prayed to the spirits to bring you back to me. This time I will kill you."

Fargo believed the stocky medicine man would try. Kills Fast didn't take up the English translation of his traditional name on a mere whim. He had killed and scalped untolled numbers of red men, Shoshoni, Crow, and Sioux alike, long before hearing the English version.

The first white he killed was Lucinda Worthy, a girl of only sixteen. Kills Fast captured her during an attack on a wagon train on South Pass in the summer of '54. After her capture, Lucinda taught him to speak

English. Then he cut her throat and added her red scalp to the long black ones that fluttered in the breeze atop his tepee poles. "Chief Many Horses isn't here to stop me from killing you this time. Pray to your God, Skye Fargo, while you feel me cut and peel off your scalp."

Fargo felt the razor-sharp edge break the skin high on his forehead.

The warriors encircling the two men nervously shifted weight to the other foot.

"I see the Trailsman's stallion," a deep voice boomed in the Cheyenne language. "Where is he?"

"Here," Fargo cried as the blade lifted.

The crowd of warriors parted. Chief Many Horses strode through the gap. He glanced at the red hairline fissure on Fargo's forehead, then looked at his medicine man and frowned.

Kills Fast explained, "These warriors caught him below the pass. Skye Fargo killed two of them." The medicine man aimed puckered lips at the two dead men surrounded by wailing women and children, then he continued. "The spirits say his penalty is death. I want his scalp."

"Wait a goddamn minute," Fargo yelled as he squirmed clear of the scalping knife. Rising onto his knees, Fargo stared into the Cheyenne chief's dark eyes and went on, "They came at me with knives and tomahawks, not handshakes."

"He came to get my white slave woman," Kills Fast hurried to add.

They watched Chief Many Horses rub his heavily wrinkled face, obviously deep in thought, pondering how to handle the two adversaries. Finally he said, "First, we go into the sweat lodge when the moon is dark. I want to listen to what the spirits have to say. Untie the Trailsman and bring him to my tepee."

Having uttered his wisdom, Many Horses turned and headed for his tepee.

Reluctantly, Kills Fast ordered two men to release Fargo. As the big man ambled away, the medicine man leveled a promise. "My blade will cut you many times, Skye Fargo. I will hang your scalp on the tip of a special tepee pole so my people will see it and remember it was their medicine man who took it from the big white man, the Trailsman."

Grim-jawed, Fargo said nothing. Two husky warriors, gripping scalping knives, with their bare arms folded across their hairless chests, blocked the big man's path. His eyes flicked from one to the other as he reached down the left Levi's pant leg and withdrew his Arkansas toothpick from its calf sheath.

Surprise washed over the warrior's faces. They glanced at each other, then at Kills Fast, as though asking him what they should do now that the white man was armed. Fargo boldly pushed the two aside and kept walking.

Behind him, Kills Fast's voice growled, "Sixty stone people, Skye Fargo, sixty. The ancient ones will weaken you with their hot breaths and take you to the brink of death. Then I will slay you."

Two other warriors darted ahead and escorted Fargo to the old chief's tepee. As one rapped on the tepee covering next to the door flap, Fargo sheathed the stiletto.

"Enter," Many Horses grunted.

Fargo pulled off his boots, bent, and stepped through the entrance. Chief Many Horses sat on buffalo robes placed in the west. Two middle-aged women, Many Horse's wives, One Feather and Pretty Grass, sat on robes in the north. One Feather broke and fed twigs to the small fire in the center of the tepee. Pretty Grass handed a gourd of water to her husband.

Neither female made eye contact with the chief's

guest, although they knew him. They were being obedient to their teachings from infancy, in this case to never look into a man's eyes—any man's, that is, other than her mate's. They did this out of respect for the man.

The fear was that even the most innocent glance could be interpreted as a signal of sexual arousement, if not by the man, then by her mate, when the trio was together. Accordingly, Cheyenne women, like all other Indian women living on the Great Plains, never looked into the eyes of another man unless her mate told her it would be all right. Even then, it was rarely done. Long-standing habits were hard to break.

Fargo knew enough Cheyenne to communicate with them. Sign language filled in the gaps. Fargo used both when saying, "Venerable Chief Many Horses honors me by asking me to sit in peace with him. It is unfortunate that two of your warriors had to die."

Many Horses replied, "What's done is done, Trailsman. They were hotheads, Kills Fast's men, not mine. Their allegiance is to the medicine man. He filled their brains with bad thoughts. When I'm away, he fans their fires of hatred for the white faces. You are lucky I returned when I did. Kills Fast hungers to claim your scalp."

"He nearly had it this time," Fargo muttered. His problem with the medicine man started before Lucinda Worthy was taken captive. Fargo was much younger then, still learning his red relatives' ways and customs. He went out of his way to make friends with as many of them as possible. He found that in order to gain their respect and acceptance, it was vital to respond in kind.

The red man's blood was the same color as his, their smiles and laughter the same. They hoped, dreamed, and feared the same as white people. In many respects, the red people were more organized, better-off than their white counterparts. The Trailsman found them to his liking.

He honed his tracking skills on hunts with them. They taught him how to use wild-creature hearing, a sixth sense common to his and their four-legged relatives, especially deer and antelope, and the phantomlike cougar.

Kills Fast, Fargo's senior by five years, was a budding medicine man back then. He had a tendency to try his big white friend's patience, test his will, probe his mind, especially quizzing him about white females. Thinking the man was truly curious, nothing more than that, Fargo told him about some of the young ladies he had bedded in San Francisco and other places. Unwittingly, he had sown a seed in Kills Fast's mind, one that would come back to haunt Fargo.

After hearing about Lucinda's demise, Fargo rode into Cheyenne country, found Kills Fast, and confronted him with the tales going around about what he did to Lucinda.

Of course, the medicine man admitted the stories were true. In fact, he was proud of what he had done. He went further, explaining and justifying, "I didn't want to hurt her. The woman made me kill her. She started showing no respect for me. I caught her in Lame Bear's tepee and killed both of them."

Fargo told him, "What did you expect her to do? Lucinda wasn't wise in the ways of Indians. You took her from her parents. Do whites steal your women? No!" Mad as hell, Fargo had warned him, "If I ever again hear that you have taken a white female captive, I'll come looking for you."

They fought an almost deadly fight with knives. Although badly wounded, Fargo's superior strength and a stronger will to survive finally bested the medicine man. Fargo pinned him to the ground. The tip of his stiletto was poised to puncture Kills Fast's jugular vein. Fargo took the stiletto away. He stood and said, "Next time, I'll send you to the spirits."

Kills Fast had answered, "No! The next time we meet, I'll have your scalp."

Chief Many Horses and all the warriors had watched the fight and heard what was said.

Fargo felt directly responsible for what happened to Lucinda Worthy. Now he wished he had gone ahead and ended Kills Fast's life. Gazing into the fire, he muttered, "He nearly had it this time." He blinked and the memory faded. Lifting his gaze onto the old man's wrinkled face, he asked in a stronger voice, "Is his latest captive well?"

Many Horses nodded, "She lives. But only barely. Kills Fast beats her." He glanced at his wives and they at him, then lowered their gazes to their folded hands in their laps.

Fargo knew they had eye-talked. After a long moment of silence, Many Horses told them to look at Fargo when telling what was on their minds.

One Feather glanced up at Fargo and said in a quiet voice, "Trailsman, the white woman's misery is great. Steal her and go."

That's precisely what he intended to do. Nodding, he asked, "Where is she? Kills Fast's tepee?"

"Yes," Pretty Grass answered. "He keeps her tied up. When Kills Fast is away, he has one of his warriors watch her."

Fargo looked at Many Horses and asked, "Do you no longer have control over your people?"

Gazing into the flames, Many Horses said, "Not much. I'm old and weak, Trailsman, and my medicine man knows it. Soon I will die. He knows this, too. He wants to be the chief. In the meantime, he lets me live."

Pretty Grass and One Feather squirmed nervously and looked at each other. They're eye-talking again,

Fargo thought. Finally, One Feather looked at her husband and suggested, "We will go into the sweat lodge with you tonight. Here is what we will do."

Fargo listened intently to the women's scheme for freeing the white woman and, at the same time, nullifying any attempt by the medicine man to prevent it from happening. He thought their plan had merit, would work, and said so. He asked only two questions: "Where will I find my rifle and Colt? And what about the horses?"

One Feather answered the first. "On Kills Fast's tepee floor just inside the door."

Pretty Grass answered the second. "Your horse will be saddled and waiting in the corral. Take any pony for her."

"Does that meet with your approval, Many Horses?" Fargo inquired.

A tired grin formed on the old man's lips as he nodded and said, "It is a wise man who councils with his women. They always know what to do. Now, we sleep, Trailsman. Preserve your strength, for you will need much this night."

Fargo watched the old man lie on his side facing the fire. One Feather covered him with a buffalo robe, then she and Pretty Grass reclined with their backs to the fire. Fargo added a handful of twigs to the embers, then he too lay down to sleep.

Somebody rapping on the tepee covering awakened him. He looked out the open doorway and saw it was dark. A warrior announced the medicine man sent him to get Skye Fargo. "The stone people are ready," he said.

Many Horses sat up, rubbed his face, and grunted, "All right, we're coming."

Fargo noticed Pretty Grass's absence. One Feather put a finger to her lips, clearly cautioning him to not speak. Her eyes followed the warrior's soft footsteps as he went around the tepee and left. Then she signed, "Pretty Grass has left to make your horse ready. She will join us at the sweat lodge."

Outside, Fargo pulled on his boots and posed two more questions. "Where is Kills Fast's tepee, and the horses?"

One Feather shot puckered lips at a black-bottomed tepee on the far side of the open space where Kills Fast had threatened him with the scalping knife.

Chief Many Horses told him the ponies and his horse were hitched to long ropes tied to trees on the north side of the encampment.

Pretty Grass met them on their way to the sweat site, located a short distance from the encampment, near a pond. Fargo and Many Horses walked side by side while the wives followed in their footprints at a discreet distance. Nobody spoke.

Kills Fast sat on the trunk of a fallen pine. The doorman and fire keeper stood near the bonfire, staring into the flames. Upon seeing Fargo, the medicine man stood and snapped his fingers. The lean firekeeper instantly began pulling sections of blazing pine logs from around the fire to expose the sixty ancient ones stacked in pyramid form. The column of stones was white-hot, transparent. Fargo knew that the cruel medicine man intended to kill him and the others with steam. In so doing, the man would kill two birds with one stone: Fargo, his enemy, and Many Horses, his chief.

Fargo went behind the low dome-shaped lodge to undress and wait for the women to crawl inside and move to sit in the north.

The medicine man entered after them and sat on the immediate north edge of the low-built doorway. Fargo knew to sit in the honor seat in the west, so he preceded Many Horses, who would sit opposite Kills Fast. All were completely nude. They looked at the shallow stone pit and watched the first seven glowing red-and-white stones come in and be ceremoniously touched by the long stem of Kills Fast's pipe, then arranged in the pit. Silence was demanded while the initial seven stones were put in place. Their silence was a show of respect. The ancient ones would die after cooling and never be used again.

While the fire-keeper and doorman shuttled back and forth, bringing in the rest of the stones, Kills Fast used the time to taunt Fargo. "So, my former friend, it comes down to this. Don't die in here, Skye Fargo. Suffer, yes, but don't die." He looked at Many Horses and said, "Remember, you were the one who asked for this sweat. I will not decide what happens to you. The spirits will." He glanced back at Fargo and continued, "If he dies, blame will be yours, Skye Fargo. We didn't invite you into our encampment."

"No, you dragged me into it," Fargo muttered.

"I know why you came. Dragging or riding makes no difference."

The sweaty face of the fire-keeper appeared in the doorway. He nodded that the rest of the stones were in the pit. Kills Fast told him to lower the door flap.

The dramatic rise in temperature was instantaneous. The bright-red mound of stones, none smaller than a large cantaloupe, cast a glow that lit the interior. Fargo and the women followed Many Horses' example as he bent and touched his nose to the moist ground, seeking cooler air to breathe in advance of what was to come.

One-half of a geode large as a buffalo skull had been put on the ground between the stone pit and the doorway. It was filled with water and had a buffalo horn in the bottom of it. Kills Fast smiled as he poured water onto the searing stones. The ancient ones crackled, hissed, and spat. The resulting blast of steam was murderously hot on Fargo's back. The two women groaned. Kills Fast dipped and poured four more hornsful in rapid succession. Fargo buried his nose in the hot, muddy ground, then willed himself not to move a muscle and took shallow breaths. Kills Fast burst out laughing and added even more water to the stones.

Pretty Grass fell onto the medicine man and clutched his arms, effectively pinning him. "Now," she cried.

Chief Many Horses dumped the entire geode of water onto the stones. A mammoth cloud of dense steam erupted. Moving swiftly through it, Fargo went one way, One Feather the other. She helped Pretty Grass hold down Kills Fast while Fargo stumbled over Many Horse's prostrate body en route to the door.

As he pushed it open, a mighty gush of pent-up steam exploded out of the opening. Fargo crawled out, closed the flap, and said to the startled warriors, "The spirits are angry. They told me to leave and for you to keep the others inside."

The doorman stepped on the bottom part of the door flap and gestured for the fire-keeper to help him. Fargo dressed as he ran back to the tepees. Knowing a guard was inside Kills Fast's tepee, he decided to flush him out. Smoke rose out of the upper vent. Fargo quickly moved the poles that held the vent flaps apart and closed them tightly. Then he dashed to and stood beside the door flap. The warrior and woman started coughing. The flap was pushed open. The warrior emerged rubbing his eyes and gagging.

Fargo's right fist slammed into the man's abdomen. A hard uppercut to the jaw and the warrior went down. He didn't get up. Fargo reached in and got his guns. The woman was tied to a tepee pole. Cutting her free, he asked, "Are you Imogene Talbot?"

"Yes," she gasped.